Witch Is When The Music Stopped

Published by Implode Publishing Ltd
© Implode Publishing Ltd 2017

Chapter 1

"You're going in early," Jack said, through a mouthful of toast.

"I'm not going into work yet. I had a phone call from Kathy while you were in the shower. She has something she wants to show me. Something exciting, she said."

"What is it?"

"No idea. She wouldn't say. It must be something pretty spectacular for her to ask me to go over at this time of the morning, though. I'll see you tonight."

I have to admit that I was intrigued. I'd tried my best to prise the information out of Kathy, but she'd been determined to build the suspense.

"So, what's so exciting that you dragged me around here at this time of the morning?" I demanded when she opened the door.

"Good morning to you too. Do you want a cup of tea?"

"I want to know what this top-secret surprise of yours is."

"Are you sure you don't want a drink? I bought a new packet of custard creams yesterday."

"Go on then. I'll have tea and biscuits, but then I want to know what you're being so secretive about."

I waited in the lounge while Kathy made us both a cup of tea.

"These are soft," I complained. There was nothing worse than a limp custard cream.

"They shouldn't be; I haven't had them twenty-four hours. They were on offer from that new shop in the precinct: 'Cheaptastic Bargains'."

I grabbed the packet. "I'm not surprised they were on offer. The sell-by date is three months ago." I took a swig of tea to wash down the offending biscuit. "So, come on, why did you get me over here? This had better be good."

"It is." Kathy's face lit up. "You stay there, and I'll go and get it."

I still had no idea what she might be up to.

Then the noise began. It sounded like — no — it couldn't be.

 But it was.

Kathy pushed the vacuum cleaner into the room, and began to vacuum the floor.

"What do you think?" she shouted.

"Is that it?"

"What?" She couldn't hear me over the noise of the vacuum.

"Is that your big surprise?" I shouted.

"What?"

"Turn it off." I gestured to her to throw the switch.

The silence was golden.

"You got me over here, at this time of the morning, just because you've got a new vacuum cleaner?"

"It's not just any old vacuum cleaner. It's one of those new ones. All very high-tech."

"I went without my breakfast to come over here, and for what? A soggy custard cream and a boring vacuum cleaner?"

"It isn't boring. I'll have you know this is the best thing since sliced bread."

"Why do people say that?"

"Say what?"

"That something is the best thing since sliced bread?"

"It's just a saying."

"It's a daft saying. Think about it. Sliced bread has been around for over a hundred years, and yet, according to you, that vacuum cleaner is the best thing to be invented since then. What about space travel? The internet? Medical advances? Custard creams?"

"Jill!"

"What?"

"You're doing it again. Going off on one. It's just a saying." She pushed the vacuum cleaner closer to me. "What do you think of it? Honestly?"

"I think it's fantastic, and I'm ecstatic that you dragged me over here to see it."

"I knew you'd like it."

Sometimes, I wondered if Kathy had missed out on the sarcasm gene.

"Where are Peter and the kids, anyway?"

"The kids stayed at Pete's Mum's last night. He's gone to pick them up. They haven't seen the new vacuum cleaner yet."

"That will be a treat for them."

"I know. To tell you the truth, I'm a bit worried about Lizzie."

"Why?"

"She has to write an essay for school about her best friend, and she says she's going to write about Caroline."

"The little ghost girl?"

"Yeah. I'm worried about what her teacher will make of it, and the other kids will probably all make fun of her. I've tried to persuade her to write about one of her real friends, but she insists that none of them is her best friend—Caroline is."

"I wouldn't worry about it. The teacher will understand that kids of Lizzie's age have a fertile imagination."

"I hope you're right."

"What about Mikey? Still banging the drums, I assume."

"I think he's starting to get tired of them." Kathy didn't try to hide her delight.

"I thought he was obsessed with them?"

"He was, but that's how it seems to go. It's all or nothing. He hasn't been down to Tom Tom for over a week now. We're keeping our fingers crossed that that particular phase has passed."

"What about all the money you've spent on the kit?"

"I'll gladly give that up if it means I don't have to listen to that row ever again. And besides, we'll probably be able to sell them."

"What's he doing instead?"

"You'll never guess."

"Football?"

"No. He asked Pete if he'd take him fishing. Pete was gobsmacked because Mikey has never shown any interest before. They went for the first time last weekend, and from all accounts, Mikey loved it."

"How does Peter feel about that? I thought it was his way of getting away from you lot."

"He seems okay with it. Pete reckons Mikey is a natural. They didn't catch many fish though."

"I thought Peter was meant to be some kind of expert fisherman."

"Only in his own mind. Typical man—he blamed it on the new factory that's opened at Wash Point."

"I didn't know they'd built one."

"It all seems to have been kept very quiet. There isn't

even a name on the building. According to Pete, there's a whole section of the river that you can no longer access because it goes through land fenced off by the factory. He's not very impressed because that was his favourite spot."

"Poor old Peter. It's good news about the drums, anyway. I suppose I'd better get going."

"Hey, Jill, do you follow the Washbridge Bloggers?"

"I've never heard of it."

"It's a community website where people who live in Washbridge can host their blogs for free."

"Not really my sort of thing. I bet it's as dull as dishwater, isn't it?"

"Usually, yes, but not recently."

"Why? Has there been some salacious gossip?"

"No. Everyone is glued to the Wizard's Wife's blog."

I didn't like the sound of that. At all. "Wizard?"

"Yeah. The woman who writes the blog is obviously a sandwich short of a picnic. She reckons that her husband is a wizard, and that she only found out recently."

"Who is she?"

"No one knows. She says she can't reveal her identity because there are people who will take her husband away if it ever comes out that he's told her he's a wizard. What did she call them? Rogue Retainers, I think."

"Retrievers."

Oh bum! Me and my big mouth!

"I thought you said you hadn't read her blog."

"I—err—I haven't."

"How come you know what they're called, then?"

"Now I come to think about it, Jules mentioned it to me the other day. The woman who writes this blog is obviously off her head, isn't she?"

"Probably, but wouldn't it be cool if it was true? Fancy being married to a real wizard. Don't you think that would be exciting?"

"About as exciting as your new vacuum cleaner." I started for the door. "I need to get going. The next time you drag me over here, I'll expect non-soggy custard creams that are still within their sell-by date."

***

On my way into the office, I was still thinking about what Kathy had said. There were probably a number of human women, living in Washbridge, who were married to wizards. Not many of them would have known their husband's secret, but I knew one who did. Jen had been struggling to keep her secret ever since Blake had revealed to her that he was a wizard. When he'd decided to come clean, I'd thought that it was a mistake, and so it had turned out. Jen was hopeless at keeping it to herself, particularly after she'd had a drink or three. I had a horrible feeling that she might be the mysterious woman behind the blog that Kathy had been reading. If so, I needed to get Blake to shut it down before the thing went viral, otherwise we'd all be in trouble.

For a moment, when I stepped into the outer office, I thought I'd developed double vision. Instead of the one reception desk, there were now two—side by side. Jules was sitting at the one closest to the door. Mrs V was seated behind the second desk.

"This isn't fair!" Jules complained, before I'd even had a chance to ask what was going on. "This is meant to be my day."

"It is your day," Mrs V said.

"Then why are you here, too?" Jules turned to me. "Tell her, Jill. Tell her it isn't fair."

"Hold on." I held up my hand to stop any further bickering. "Why doesn't someone tell me what's going on? Maybe you should start by explaining why there are two desks in here."

"You'd better ask her." Jules pouted.

"It's really very simple," Mrs V said. "I've handed in my notice at Wheels On Meals."

"Wheelie?"

"Jill!" Mrs V tutted. "Do you have to do that?"

"Sorry, I couldn't resist it one last time. What happened? I thought you liked working there?"

"I did at first, but then I realised that some of the wheelies are only in it for the adrenaline buzz."

"What do you mean?"

"They're far more interested in setting new speed records for delivering the meals than they are about the service they provide. They were being downright reckless. When I saw poor old Mr Earnshaw's Yorkshire pudding fall off his plate, I'd had enough. I told the manager, but he did nothing about it, so I handed in my notice."

"I'm sorry to hear that, but it still doesn't explain the additional desk."

"I can't stay at home, Jill. I simply can't. I didn't know what to do, but then I had a brainwave."

"Huh!" Jules rolled her eyes.

Mrs V continued. "Everyone knows that two heads are better than one, so I thought what's to stop you having two PAs?"

"We don't need two," Jules interrupted. "It's not like we have many clients, is it?"

"Thanks for that, Jules," I said. "I still don't understand where the second desk came from."

"That was courtesy of Armi." Mrs V beamed. "He's such a little darling. I told him what I was thinking of doing, and he said that there were plenty of desks going spare at Armitage, Armitage, Armitage and Poole. He got some of his people to bring it over here."

"No one consulted me!" Jules was obviously more than a little put out about this new arrangement. "She's undermining my position!"

Oh boy! Why was nothing ever simple?

"I need you two to call a truce. We'll have to see how this thing works out. For now, whoever's day it 'should' be, can sit at the desk closest to the outer door, and deal with any clients. Okay?"

"That's fine by me." Mrs V smiled.

"I suppose so." Jules didn't.

***

I hurried through to my office where I found Winky sitting on the floor, with his back to me. Before I could wish him good morning, he began to speak.

To the wall.

"Red? Me too. I hate the pink stuff. What about milk? Really? Me too. Full cream, every time."

"Err—Winky?" I interrupted.

He turned around. "Morning. Sorry, I didn't hear you come in."

"Why were you talking to the wall?"

"To the—?" He grinned. "Of course. You can't see Lenny, can you?"

"Who's Lenny?"

"An old friend of mine—now sadly departed."

"I don't follow."

"For someone who is so embroiled with the supernatural world, you're pretty slow on the uptake, aren't you? Lenny is a ghost."

I looked over at the wall. "You're saying there's a ghost over there? I can't sense it. I usually can."

"That's probably because you're only tuned into human ghosts."

"Oh? Lenny is a cat?"

"Of course he is." Winky turned back to the wall. "Lenny, attach yourself to this two-legged, would you? What? No, it's okay. She's used to seeing ghosts."

"Can you see me now?" the ghostly-looking tabby said.

"Yeah. Hi, Lenny."

"Hi. I'm not used to speaking to two-leggeds. I used to live with humans, so I never got the chance to talk to them."

"Have you been a ghost for long?"

"Only a week. I never saw that bus coming."

"Ouch! Nasty! I'm sorry to hear that."

"That's okay. I can get around much easier now that I'm a ghost because I don't have to worry about dogs. Only the ghost dogs, and there aren't many of those around here. I thought I'd take the opportunity to catch up with my old mucker, Winky. It's been a long time, hasn't it, pal?"

"Too long." Winky turned to me. "Where are your manners? How about offering our guest some salmon?"

"I suppose you'll be joining him?"

"Naturally. Red, not pink."

"Obviously."

Chapter 2

How?

That was the question I was asking myself. How did my life ever become so crazy? So far that morning: I'd had my sister drag me half way across town at the break of dawn, just to see a stupid vacuum cleaner, and I now had not one, but two PAs, sitting in my outer office. And just to top it off, there was a ghost cat eating salmon and drinking full cream milk in my office.

I needed to get out of there, to find a little oasis of sanity.

So why, oh why, did I choose to magic myself over to Cuppy C?

"You can serve *her*." Amber turned her back on me. "I'm not speaking to her."

"I'm not speaking to her either," Pearl said.

"Come on, you two. I'm really sorry." I hadn't seen the twins since our weekend in London. In truth, I'd deliberately kept a low profile in the hope that things would blow over. Some chance! "How was I supposed to know that you two didn't realise how slowly the London Eye turned?"

"You should have warned us before we had those bubble teas!" Amber turned to face me.

"And those giant cokes!" Pearl said.

"It never occurred to me." I tried, but failed to stifle a laugh, as I remembered that day. The ride on the London Eye had been the last thing we did before we set off back home.

"I was bursting to go by the time we were half way around!" Amber said.

"I don't know how I managed to hang on." Pearl cringed

at the memory.

"I'm really, really sorry," I said, straight-faced. "But apart from the London Eye issue, the rest of the weekend was okay, wasn't it?"

"Except the part when you left us behind on the tube."

"That wasn't intentional."

The twins had been so overwhelmed by the London Underground that when the train arrived, they just stood back and watched. I'd assumed they had followed me onboard, and by the time I realised they were still standing on the platform, it was too late — the doors had closed and the train had started to move.

"We lost an hour because of that," Pearl said.

"That's only because you didn't do what I told you to."

"So, it was our fault, was it?" Pearl looked more than a little put out.

"When I rang you, I told you to stay put, and that I'd get on the next train back to you. But what did you do?"

"We thought you wanted us to come to you."

The twins and I had spent the best part of an hour travelling back and forth between Covent Garden and Piccadilly Circus before we were eventually reunited.

"Okay, but apart from the London Eye issue, and the Tube, the rest of the weekend was okay, wasn't it?"

"You shouldn't have let us spend so much money," Pearl said.

"How was I supposed to stop you? Once you got onto Oxford Street, you were like two women possessed."

"You should have kept us in check. Alan and William went ballistic when they saw what we'd bought."

"I tried to get you to rein it in, but you weren't in any mood to listen to me. But, apart from the London Eye issue, the Tube, and the over-spending, the rest of the weekend was okay, wasn't it?"

"I suppose so," Amber conceded. "I enjoyed watching Changing the Guard."

"I enjoyed the boat trip to Greenwich." Pearl smiled for the first time since I'd arrived.

"Me too." Much to my surprise, the weekend in London hadn't been quite the ordeal I'd feared. Apart from the Tube and London Eye incidents, everything had gone remarkably well, considering.

I was just about to order a latte and a muffin when I spotted Maria, Luther's ex-girlfriend, across the road.

"Jill? Don't you want anything?" Amber called after me, but I was already halfway out of the door.

It took me a couple of minutes to catch up with Maria.

"Jill? Where did you come from?"

"I was in Cuppy C."

"I've just been doing a spot of shopping." She held up three carrier bags.

"So I see. I was hoping I might bump into you sooner or later."

"Oh? Why?"

"Can't you guess?"

"Luther?"

"He's pretty upset by the way you dumped him."

"I feel terrible about it. He's a great guy, but what could I do? The temptation to drink human blood was much greater than I ever imagined. I was terrified I'd forget myself, and sink my fangs into his neck."

I cringed at the thought. "Is there nothing I can say to change your mind?"

"Not unless you can come up with some way that I can be with Luther without feeling the constant craving for human blood."

"That's a big ask, but I'll give it some thought. Will you give me your telephone number, in case I need to get in touch with you?"

"Sure."

***

While I'd been talking to Maria, Cuppy C had got much busier; the queue now stretched right back to the door. I couldn't be bothered to wait, so I made my way over to Aunt Lucy's house instead.

"Lovely to see you, Jill."

"I just called in at Cuppy C."

"Did the twins give you a hard time?" She grinned. "I heard what happened on that big wheel thing."

"I think they've forgiven me now."

"I'm glad you came over because I've got something really exciting to show you."

"Oh? What's that?"

"Just wait there." She hurried out of the room before I could ask any more questions.

"Ready?" she called, a few seconds later.

"Yeah."

"Prepare to be amazed."

"Okay."

Oh no! I couldn't believe my ears.

Aunt Lucy came back into the lounge, pushing a vacuum cleaner. It was exactly the same model as the one that Kathy had shown me earlier.

"What do you think?" Aunt Lucy switched it off.

"It's—err—very exciting."

"Isn't it just? It's ten times more powerful than my old one."

"Ten times, eh? That's—err—great. Anyway, I only popped in to say 'hello'. I'd better be going."

"Don't rush off. There's something I wanted to talk to you about. I need a favour, actually."

"What's that?"

"A friend of mine, Rhoda Riddle, came to see me yesterday. She knows that you're a P.I, and she thought you might be able to help."

"With what?"

"Her son, Robbie, has gone missing."

"Here in Candlefield?"

"Yes. At least, I think so. They're pixies. Pixies rarely travel to the human world because their height makes it impossible for them to mix with humans without being noticed."

"I don't think I've ever met a pixie. How tall are they?"

"Typically, no taller than six inches."

"What's the story with her son?"

"I don't know the details. Rhoda was so upset that it was difficult to make much sense of what she was saying. I do have her address, though. Would you call around there and talk to her?"

"Of course. I'll go now."

"Before you do, Hamlet said he wanted a word with you, the next time you came over."

"Did he?" Great. That sounded like trouble. "I suppose I'd better go and see what he wants. Where's Barry, by the way?"

"He's over at Dolly's house. She took him for a walk last night, and said she'd bring him back today."

Hamlet was in his cage, seated in a miniature armchair. He was wearing a maroon smoking jacket.

"So funny." He chuckled. He was reading a book, but I couldn't see the cover. "Have you read much Wodehouse, Jill?"

"No."

"You should. You really should."

"I understand you want to see me about something."

"That's right. I have the opportunity to take a vacation overseas."

"You do? How?"

"The Hamster Travel Group. I joined a short while ago."

"Where will you be going?"

"On a cruise. Around the Caribbean."

"Nice. Isn't that expensive?"

"It's subsidised. Before I can go, though, I'll need a passport."

"Right?"

"I thought you could organise that for me."

"I wouldn't know where to begin."

"First, you'll need to take a photo of me. You can do that on your phone."

"Okay."

"Then, I'll need you to collect a rodent passport form."

"Where would I get one of those?"

"I'll give you one guess."

"Everything Rodent?"

"Got it in one. If you let me have the form, I can take it from there."

"Okay."

Sheesh! If I wasn't running around after cats or dogs, it was hamsters. My life just wasn't my own.

**

It took me a while to find the houses where Aunt Lucy's friend, Rhoda, lived. Pixie Court was in the Pixie Central area of Washbridge where all the buildings were tiny.

The roof of her house only came up to my knee, so I was forced to get down on all-fours in order to knock at the tiny red door.

"Hello?" The female pixie looked up at me.

"Are you Rhoda Riddle?"

"That's me. You must be Jill. Lucy said she was going to ask you to come over."

"I understand your son has gone missing?"

"That's right. Would you like a drink? The cups will be rather small for you, I'm afraid."

"No, I'm okay, thanks."

"Do you have much experience in finding missing pixies?"

"I have to be honest. This is my first pixie-related case. I have had some experience in tracking down missing persons in the human world, though. When did Robbie go missing?"

"Three days ago."

"How old is he?"

"Twenty. He's in his last year at college."

"Is it possible that he's with a friend? Or a girlfriend?"

"Robbie is engaged to a wonderful girl named Maddy. I've already checked with her; she's just as worried as I am. We've contacted all of his friends too. No one has seen him.

This isn't like Robbie, Jill. He's hardly ever late in, and if he is going to be, he always lets me know."

"Where was he, the last time you saw him?"

"He left the house around midday on Saturday. He told me he was going to meet Lionel—he's one of Robbie's friends, but when I checked, Lionel said he hadn't seen Robbie, and that they'd never arranged to meet that day."

"Robbie lied to you?"

"It seems that way, but Robbie never lies. I'm really worried, Jill."

"Understandably. I'll need a recent photograph of Robbie, and a list of all his friends."

"Of course. I can have that ready in an hour."

"Could you possibly drop the photo and info off at Aunt Lucy's? I'll pick it up from there later."

"No problem. Do you think you'll be able to find him?"

"I'll do my best. In the meantime, try not to worry. I'm sure he'll be okay."

***

Bill Ratman was behind the counter at Everything Rodent.

"Hello, young lady. It's been a while since we've seen you in here. How's—err—whatshisname?"

"Hamlet. He's fine, thanks. He was reading Wodehouse when I left him."

"Ah, yes. Jeeves is quite popular with the hamsters. Now, what can I do for you, today?"

"I understand that you have rodent passport application forms?"

"We do."

"Good."

"Normally."

My heart sank. "Normally?"

"We're all out at the moment. I'm waiting for a fresh batch from the Rodent Passport Authority. If you have the time to pop over there, you could pick up some for me."

This was beginning to feel a lot like déjà vu.

"Before I go over there, are you sure they're stocked up with toner cartridges? I don't want a repeat of what happened when I went to get the Rodent Match forms."

"Oh, yes." He grinned. "I'd forgotten all about that. You have nothing to worry about this time, though. They bought three new toners only ten days ago."

"Okay. You'd better give me directions then."

Chapter 3

I fell for it every time. Bill Ratman at Everything Rodent had assured me that the Rodent Passport Authority would have the forms, but they were all out of them. To make matters worse, they couldn't print any more because—wait for it. No, they weren't out of toner cartridges; they were out of paper. And guess who they bought their paper from? You got it—Everything Rodent. Ninety minutes later, and I was exhausted. I'd been back to Everything Rodent to collect the paper, and then back to the Rodent Passport Authority where I'd had to wait while they printed the forms. Once I had those, I'd made yet another trip to Everything Rodent, to drop them off, and then went back to Aunt Lucy's.

"There you go, Hamlet." I held out the form.

"I don't need it now." He barely looked up from his book. "I've just heard that the cruise has been cancelled. I hope you didn't go to too much trouble."

"Trouble?" I had to bite my lip. "No, not at all."

***

I magicked myself back to Washbridge, and as I made my way to the office, I noticed several posters that featured the picture of a chameleon. The wording simply read: *Chameleon – coming soon! Prepare to be amazed.* It was all very intriguing, but gave no clue as to what it was about.

The atmosphere in the outer office was still frosty. It was obvious that Mrs V and Jules weren't talking; they weren't even looking at one another. I would have to sort out that situation sooner or later, but after my rodent exploits, I wasn't in the mood for it right then.

"What's going on out there?" Winky was sitting on my desk.

"What do you mean?"

"I realise that you're not the most observant person in the world, but even you must have spotted there are two desks out there?"

"It's nothing. Just a storm in a teacup."

"What are you going to do about it?"

"I don't know."

"That's your problem, right there. You're too indecisive."

"No, I'm not. Am I? Maybe, I am. I don't know."

"I rest my case. It's obvious what you should do."

"What's that?"

"Sack the old bag lady. I've been telling you that for ages. Jules is much more pleasing to the eye."

"That's ageist."

"No, it isn't. It's ugliest. Let's be honest, the old bag lady is well past her sell-by date."

"Just like Kathy's custard creams."

"What?"

"Nothing. It doesn't matter. And, no, I'm not getting rid of Mrs V. She may not be in her prime, but she has bags of experience, and you can't put a price on that."

"Is that why you don't pay her? Because you can't put a price on it?"

Just then, there was a commotion in the outer office. Moments later, my door burst open, and both Jules and Mrs V tried to step inside. Unfortunately, the gap wasn't wide enough to accommodate them both at the same time, so they became wedged in the doorway.

"What's going on?" I was rapidly losing patience with them.

"You have a visitor, Jill," they said, in almost perfect harmony.

I wasn't expecting anyone. Not that day, or the next, or the next or — you get the picture.

"Who is it?"

"Sheila Bowlings," Jules blurted out.

"A Mrs Bowlings," Mrs V said.

"Okay. Will *one* of you please send her in?"

It took a few seconds for them to dislodge themselves from the doorway, but then both women disappeared back into the outer office. When they returned, Mrs V was leading the way, followed by the client who was in turn followed by Jules. It looked as though they might break into the conga at any moment.

"Thanks, Jules, Mrs V. That will be all."

"I've never known anyone have two receptionists before." Mrs Bowlings looked understandably puzzled.

"It's an experiment."

"They both tried to give me a scarf, but I told them that I'm allergic to wool. It brings me out in hives."

"Nasty. Won't you have a seat? Can I get you a drink?"

"Not for me, thanks."

That came as something of a relief. The last thing I needed was Jules and Mrs V fighting over who would make it.

"How can I help you, Mrs Bowlings?"

"Call me Sheila. My husband has gone missing."

Two missing person cases in the same day? That was a first.

"When and where did he go missing?"

"Brendan, that's his name, went fishing on Friday. That was the last time I saw him."

"That's only a few days ago. Does he sometimes stay away from home?"

"Never. Brendan is a home bird. I don't remember the last time he spent the night away. He's usually back from fishing by seven o' clock. Eight at the very latest."

"Does he have a phone? Have you tried calling him?"

"He does, and I have, but it seems to be switched off."

"Where does he go fishing?"

"To Wash Point."

"My brother-in-law fishes there."

"Brendan has been going there for years. He loves his fishing."

"Have you spoken to the police?"

"Yes—twice now, but they're not interested. They said to go back if he hasn't turned up in a week's time. They say this sort of thing happens all the time, and that I shouldn't worry."

"It's true that most 'missing' people turn up under their own steam within a couple of days."

"Brendan would never go off anywhere without letting me know. He knows how much I worry."

"I'm sorry to have to ask this, Sheila, but have the two of you been having any problems, lately? Any arguments?"

"No, nothing like that. Our marriage is solid. We hardly ever have a cross word."

"Okay. Sorry, but I had to ask. Where does your husband work?"

"He works for the council—in Weights and Measures. It's all he has ever done."

"What about friends? Fishing buddies?"

"Brendan doesn't really have any friends. The only time he ever goes out is with me, or when he goes fishing alone. I know he chats to some of the other fishermen, but I don't know their names."

"When he left home on Friday, did he seem his normal self?"

"He was just the same as usual." She'd managed to hold it together until then, but now tears began to run down her cheeks. "He kissed me, and told me he loved me. Just like he always does."

"Do you have a photograph of your husband that you could email to me?"

"Yes. I'll do it as soon as I get home."

After she'd left, it occurred to me that it might be worth asking Peter about Brendan Bowlings. They both went fishing in the same spot. Perhaps Peter would know him.

***

Twenty minutes later, my office door opened, and in walked my two PAs. Between them, they were carrying a large package, wrapped in brown paper.

"Where do you want this?" Mrs V said. "It's heavy."

"Anywhere. Just drop it on the floor. Thanks."

I waited until they were back in the outer office before I started to unwrap it. As far as I was aware, I wasn't expecting anything.

"Huh? Moonlight Gym?" The A5 glossy flyers had obviously been delivered to the wrong address. I double-checked the label, but it was definitely addressed to me.

Winky suddenly appeared at my side. "They didn't take as long as I'd expected."

"Are these for you?"

"They most certainly are." He took the one I was holding, and began to study it. "They've made an excellent job of them, don't you think?"

"Why were they addressed to me?"

"Because your name is on the credit card, of course."

"Silly me. I should have known. What's Moonlight Gym, anyway?"

"My new business venture. It's guaranteed to make my fortune."

"Oh no you don't. You're not turning my office into a gym, even if it is only open during the night." I'd established that much from the flyer. The Moonlight Gym was scheduled to open between the hours of midnight and five in the morning. "No one is going to go to a gym at that hour."

"How little you know."

"There's no address on the flyer. How will they know where to go?"

"That's simple. They call the number on the bottom, and that gives them all the information they need."

"It had better not be based in this office."

"I'm not going to use your office. Why won't you believe me?"

"Maybe it has something to do with your track record. It isn't that long ago that you turned my office into a knitwear factory."

"Fear not. Your office is safe."

"I can check. I'll call the number on the flyer."

"Good luck with that. The message is in feline code."

"What's that?"

"I could tell you, but then I'd be forced to kill you."

Drat! Foiled again.

***

It had been a long day, what with one thing and another. I still hadn't sorted out the Mrs V/Jules situation, but I couldn't face it right then. I'd tackle that another day.

Jack wasn't home when I got back to the house. That gave me the chance to check out the blog that Kathy had told me about. It wasn't difficult to find. The blogs on the Washbridge Bloggers website were listed in order of popularity. The Wizard's Wife's blog was number one by some considerable margin.

I searched for the very first post. I had a good idea of the date when Blake had told Jen his secret. If the blog had been started before then, it was unlikely to be Jen's. Unfortunately, the dates more or less coincided. The blog had been started about five days after Blake had told Jen that he was a wizard. That didn't bode well.

Thirty minutes later, I was sure that it was Jen's blog. I could quite clearly hear her 'voice' in the posts published on the blog. The words she used, and her turn of phrase — all of them left me in no doubt that Jen was behind this. What a disaster! Blake should never have told her. If this blog went viral, then every sup living in Washbridge would be in trouble. Did Blake know Jen was doing this? I highly doubted it. I had to tell him, and I had to make sure that he got her to stop. Immediately.

"So? What was it?" Jack said, as soon as he arrived home.
"What was what?"
"The exciting thing that Kathy wanted to show you? I

thought you might have sent a text to tell me."

"It was a vacuum cleaner."

"Are you being serious?"

"Deadly. She dragged me all the way over there to look at her new vacuum cleaner. And then, just to make things even worse, her custard creams were soggy." I gave Jack a kiss. "How was your day? It can't have been any worse than mine."

"It wasn't much better. The criminals must all be on holiday this week. I spent most of the day investigating a break-in at a fish and chip shop."

"What did they steal?"

"They didn't. They forced their way in from the rear of the building. They had to partially demolish a wall to get in."

"But they didn't take anything?"

"No, but that might be because they'd got their bearings wrong. The shop next door is a jeweller. We think that was their intended target."

"They broke into the wrong shop?"

"Never underestimate the stupidity of the criminal mind." Jack dropped his newspaper onto the coffee table. "I'm going to take a shower. I stink of fish, chips and mushy peas."

When he'd gone upstairs, I noticed the headline on The Bugle, which read: An Icy End. It was the tragic story of a man who worked at the local cold store. He'd somehow managed to get himself locked in the deep freeze, and had frozen to death.

Chapter 4

"Why do you have to go in early?" I asked Jack while trying to decide between toast, porridge or cornflakes for breakfast.

"I have to interview the owner of the fish and chip shop. He's an early riser, apparently."

"Where are you interviewing him? His *plaice* or yours?" I laughed.

Jack gave me a puzzled look.

"Plaice? Get it?"

He just sighed.

"Oh my *cod*! You're no fun anymore." I laughed again.

"You need help, Jill."

"You'd *batter* hurry up or you'll be late."

"No more, please. There's a limit to how many of your terrible puns I can take in the morning."

"You're no fun. When I met you, I thought you *haddock* a sense of humour."

He rolled his eyes. "Talking of fun. I've been thinking."

"Steady on. That's twice in one week."

"We should get away more."

"We've already got a holiday booked."

"I'm talking about short breaks—long weekends—that kind of thing."

That wasn't a bad idea. I was all for long weekends spent in luxury hotels. I enjoyed being pampered.

"I was thinking that we should get a caravan," he said.

"Do what?"

"That way we can get away whenever we want. No need to book in advance. We just wait until the weather is good, hitch the caravan, and off we go."

"A caravan?"

"Yeah. It'll be great."

"A caravan?"

"It needn't be all that expensive. There are some bargains to be had."

"A caravan?"

"What do you think?"

"I think I'd rather tie myself to the back of a car with a rope, and let you drag me down the road."

"What's wrong with a caravan?"

"It's a small tin box on wheels."

"Rubbish. Caravans have all mod-cons these days. They're a home from home."

"A tin home. On wheels."

"I've sent for a brochure. You'll soon change your mind when you see just how well equipped they are nowadays. Anyway, I'd better get going." He gave me a quick peck on the lips. "I'll see you tonight."

A caravan? Not happening—not on my watch.

I had hoped to catch Blake on his own before he went to work, but by the time I'd had breakfast and was ready to leave, his car had already gone.

"Jill! Hi!" Jen came scurrying across the road.

"Morning. Has Blake left already?"

"Yeah. He has some work he needs to catch up on."

"Jack too. He has an urgent appointment at a fish and chip shop."

"Sorry?"

"It's just a case he's working on. How are you, anyway? You're looking very chipper."

"Blake and I are getting on so much better these days. I

feel much more relaxed."

"That's good. I need to chill out more, too. I should find a new hobby. I seem to spend most of my time surfing the Net. Do you spend much time online, Jen?"

"Me? No. Hardly any. And, I never blog."

"Blog?"

"In case you were wondering. I don't. Blog. Ever."

"Me neither. I've never understood what people find to talk about in blogs."

"Oh? Is that the time?" She made a show of glancing at her watch. "I have to run. Bye, Jill."

"Bye."

If there had been any doubt before, there wasn't now. Jen was definitely the mysterious Wizard's Wife blogger.

I was just about to get into the car when I heard Mrs Rollo calling to me.

"Jill, I'm glad I've caught you."

"Morning, Mrs Rollo."

"I have some exciting news."

"Have you bought a new vacuum cleaner, by any chance?"

"Sorry?"

"Never mind. What's your exciting news?"

"I've decided to go to Australia with Marco."

"Wow! That really is exciting."

"It was so good to see him. I couldn't bear the thought of us being parted again so soon."

"How long will you be going for?"

"I don't know. Six months initially, but then who knows. I might stay there."

"What about the house?"

"I'm going to rent it out for now. If I do decide to stay down-under, then I'll sell it. That's why I wanted to catch you. I'll be leaving tomorrow. I'm meeting up with Marco in York. We're going to spend some time travelling around the UK together, and then off we go to Australia. The rental people said they'd have no trouble letting this place, so you may have new neighbours soon."

"We'll miss you, Mrs Rollo."

"I'm going to miss you and Jack, too. I guess you'll have to learn to bake now."

"I suppose so."

"Come here." She pulled me into her arms, and gave me a hug. "Take care of yourself, Jill."

"You too."

I would definitely miss Mrs Rollo, but not her cakes.

***

"Morning, Jill."

I could hear Mr Ivers' voice coming from inside the toll booth, but I could barely make out his face. It took me a few moments to work out what was going on, but then I realised that someone had stuck bottle tops—dozens of them—onto the inside of the glass. Mr Ivers was peering through them.

"What do you think of my collection?" He slid open the window, so I could see him.

"You collect bottle tops?"

"I most certainly do. I'm a topper, and proud of it."

"Since when?"

"I only started recently. I stumbled across a shop in town, and since then I've been hooked."

"What made you decide to stick them to the windows of the toll booth? Don't they get in the way?"

"Not at all. It gets tiresome having people stare in at you all day long. It's like being in a goldfish bowl. This gives me some privacy. And besides, these are only my dupes."

"Dupes?"

"Duplicates. The less expensive tops are sold by the bagful, which means that you often end up with duplicates."

"I see. That's fascinating." Why was I listening to this rubbish?

"It really is, Jill. I never thought I'd say this, but I'm seriously considering packing in the movie newsletter, and starting one aimed at toppers. But don't worry, I'll give my existing subscribers a discount to encourage them to swap over."

"I might have to cancel. I'm not really into bottle tops."

"Neither was I. Until I walked into that shop, I'd never given them a second thought. Now, it's all I think about twenty-four seven."

There weren't words to describe how sad that sentence was.

***

I wasn't looking forward to getting to the office because Mrs V and Jules would no doubt still be at each other's throats. I needed to have it out with them once and for all; I just wasn't sure how I was going to play it. Telling Mrs V that she'd have to remove the 'additional' desk wouldn't go down well, but then telling Jules that she'd have to put up with Mrs V every day wasn't going to be any easier. As soon as I started up the stairs, I could hear the two of them.

But wait! They weren't yelling at one another. They were laughing.

What was going on?

"Morning, Jill." Mrs V greeted me with a smile.

"Morning." Jules beamed.

"Morning, both of you."

"Beautiful morning, isn't it?" Mrs V said.

"Would you like a drink, Jill?" Jules stood up. "I was just about to make one for Annabel and myself."

Annabel? Since when did Jules call Mrs V, Annabel? Even *I* didn't call her that.

"A cup of tea would be nice."

"One and two-thirds sugar, Jill?" Jules looked at Mrs V, and they both sniggered.

"Err—yes, please."

"Actually, dear," Mrs V said. "We were just talking about you, weren't we, Jules?"

Jules giggled.

"I happened to mention to Jules that you had a favourite rubber band."

They both laughed.

"And, I told Annabel that you also had a favourite paperclip," Jules said.

At that, the two of them broke into fits of laughter.

"I'm pleased to know that I am such a source of amusement, but I'm intrigued, what happened? Yesterday, you were at each other's throats."

"We realised that we actually enjoy working together." Mrs V wiped the tears of laughter from her eyes.

"It's much better now." Jules was slopping tea all over the table. "We get to talk about knitting all day long, don't we Annabel?"

"And crochet."

I took the cup and saucer from Jules. "So, you're both happy with this arrangement now?"

They nodded.

"Jules will come in three days a week as before," Mrs V said. "I'll come in most days unless Armi has anything planned."

"Okay." I took a sip of tea. "We'll give it a go, and see how it works out, but you'll have to decide who is going to be the receptionist for the day. It's too confusing for the clients if you both try to attend to the same person. Likewise with the scarves; it's overwhelming if both of you offer the client one."

"Don't worry, Jill," Mrs V said. "We'll sort it out between us."

"That's great." I started for my office.

"Jill," Jules called after me. "Do you have any idea what your grandmother's new product is?"

"I didn't know she had one."

"You must have seen the posters. The ones with the chameleon on them?"

"They're Grandma's? I've seen a few of them, but I didn't realise they were for Ever."

"It's being launched later today. We were both wondering — err — if — err — "

"You both want to go to the launch?"

They nodded.

"Okay. I suppose so, but no more than thirty minutes."

"Thanks, Jill." They choroused.

Winky didn't even acknowledge me when I walked into

my office. He was on the sofa, with his head buried inside a glossy brochure.

"*Morning, Jill*." I did my best Winky impression. "*How are you?* I'm very well, Winky. Thanks for asking."

He looked up. "You do know they'll come and take you away if you insist on talking to yourself, don't you?"

"It would just be nice to get a 'hello'."

"Hello," he said, and then went back to his brochure.

"What's so fascinating?"

"Just look at these babes."

For a horrible moment, I thought he was ogling a lingerie brochure, but then I realised he was looking at cars. Not just any old cars—these were luxury sports cars, which must have cost at least a hundred thousand pounds.

"They're very nice, but why are you looking at them?"

"I'm trying to decide which one I should buy."

"Yeah, right." I laughed. "And where are you going to find that kind of money?"

"With this." He held up a ticket.

"The Lottery?"

"It's a triple rollover. Thirty million for the winner. And this, is going to be the winning ticket."

"You do realise that you have more chance of being struck by lightning than you do of winning first prize?"

"And that's precisely why you'll never win anything. It's all about the positivity. Me? I'm Mr Positive. And you're little Miss Negative."

"If you say so."

He went back to the brochure. "I can't decide between the red or the black."

"Okay. Good luck with that. In the meantime, I have work to do."

"Well, they do say a change is as good as a rest."
Cheek!

Chapter 5

An hour later, Winky still had his head stuck in the car brochure. The poor deluded fool was still planning how to spend his lottery winnings. At least, he seemed to have dropped the idea of running a gym out of my office. There was no way I would have stood for that nonsense.

I needed to speak with Peter to check if he knew Brendan Bowlings — the man who had disappeared after going fishing at Wash Point. I tried to call him, but the call went to voicemail, so I left a message asking him to get back to me.

"Madeline is here to see you, Jill." Jules' voice came through the intercom.

"Send her through, would you?"

Mad had dyed her hair lime green.

"I like what you've done with your hair."

"Liar. My boss isn't too impressed. Apparently, lime green hair does not portray the right image for a librarian."

"Do you have to get it re-dyed?"

"No chance. He can kiss my butt. I think it suits me."

"Have your mum and Nails made up yet?"

"No, and Mum's taking it pretty badly."

"That surprises me. I thought she was the one who kicked him out?"

"She did, but she still loves him. Don't ask me why."

"Is she going to take him back?"

"Not unless he can prove to her that he's over his addiction to bottle tops. Anyway, the reason I dropped by was to check when you want to make a start on the training?"

"I'm not convinced there's any point to it."

"I thought you'd told Aubrey Chance that you'd give it a go?"

"I did, but it just seems like such a waste of time. No witch has ever been able to travel to Ghost Town."

"Aubrey told me that there had been one."

"He's talking about Magna Mondale, and as far as I'm aware, that's only a rumour."

"You have to at least give it a try, or Aubrey is going to be on my back."

"Okay, but I'm pretty busy at the moment. Lots of people are disappearing."

"Maybe we could get together one evening. It needn't take more than an hour or so."

"Fair enough. Can I give you a call to set something up?"

"Sure. I'm free most evenings—that's how sad my life is."

***

"We're just off, Jill." Jules popped her head around my door.

"Where to?"

"To Ever. We told you this morning."

"Oh, yeah. The Chameleon thingy. Hold on. I'm going to come with you. I'll lock the office for half an hour."

I'd probably regret this, but curiosity had got the better of me.

"It's exciting, isn't it, Jill?" Jules could barely contain herself, as we walked down the high street.

"Yeah. Almost as exciting as a new vacuum cleaner."

"Huh?"

"Never mind." I spotted the crowd gathered outside

Ever. "It looks like there's going to be a good turnout."

"Wool TV is here." Mrs V pointed.

The doors to the shop had been locked, but everyone seemed to be fascinated by something in the window.

"Can you see anything, Jill?" Jules was standing on tiptoe.

"Nothing."

"Make way for an old lady." Mrs V pushed her way through the crowd. Jules and I followed in her wake.

"It's some kind of lizard." Jules stared at the creature in the shop window. "Any idea what kind it is, Jill?"

"Duh! A chameleon, maybe?"

"Oh yes, of course."

Just then, I caught sight of Kathy, standing behind the counter. She gave me a wave.

"Ladies and gentlemen!" Grandma's voice came through the speakers which had been fixed above the door and window. "Welcome to the launch of Chameleon Wool."

The doors opened, and there, standing behind a table, was the woman herself. The crowd cheered, as if a movie star had suddenly appeared.

"Thank you for coming today. From the same people who brought you Everlasting Wool and One-Size Needles, Ever A Wool Moment is pleased to announce our latest innovative product. I give you—" And from somewhere, I kid you not, there was a drumroll. What a showman she was. "Chameleon Wool."

From behind her back, she produced a small ball of wool, and placed it in the centre of the table. The sense of anti-climax was palpable as everyone stared at this unremarkable ball of wool.

"The problem with conventional wool." Grandma

continued, seemingly unfazed by the audience's initial response. "Is that you have to buy a separate ball of wool for each colour you require." She paused for dramatic effect. "No longer!" From under the table, she produced what appeared to be a handful of patterns. "If you want the wool to be this shade of red." She held up the first pattern for everyone to see. "Then the wool will turn red." Grandma touched the ball of wool to the pattern, and it instantly turned red. There was a collective gasp as people realised what Chameleon Wool actually was. Next, she touched the same ball of wool to a pattern for a yellow cardigan. The ball of wool changed from red to yellow. That did it. Everyone cheered and screamed.

Everyone except me.

"When can we buy it?" someone behind me yelled.

"Patience." Grandma smiled, triumphantly. "You'll be able to buy Chameleon Wool as soon as this table has been cleared away. I'll just need to close the door for a few minutes. Please form an orderly queue."

"Can we stay and buy some, Jill?" Jules pleaded.

"Please, Jill." Mrs V had already joined the queue. "They might sell out otherwise."

"Okay. Get back to the office as soon as you can."

I was the only person who hadn't joined the queue. Takings were going to be through the roof at Ever, today. Chameleon Wool had certainly captured the imagination. Of course, I was the only one there who knew the truth. This was yet another example of Grandma's blatant disregard for the rules governing the use of magic in the human world. But who was going to stop her? Not the rogue retrievers, and certainly not Department V.

***

When I arrived back at the office, Peter was waiting at the top of the stairs.

"You called me. I was in town anyway, so I thought I'd drop in."

"Sorry I wasn't here. We had an office outing to Ever A Wool Moment. Jules and Mrs V are still down there."

"Kathy said something about a new product launch. She wasn't looking forward to it."

I unlocked the door, and led the way through to my office.

"I see you still have the ugly cat."

Winky, who was sitting on the sofa, scowled at Peter. "Get back to your glass house."

Fortunately, Peter didn't speak 'cat', and he continued, "Are you looking for a new car, Jill?" He picked up the brochure, which Winky had left on the floor. "Business must be good if you can afford one of these."

"That isn't mine. It belongs to—err—a—err—client."

"I had to nip into town to see the bank manager. I need to up the company's overdraft to cover the additional outlay on the Washbridge House contract."

"How's that going?"

"It's early days, but very promising. If we get this right, it should open a lot of doors."

"That's great. You'll soon be able to employ Kathy."

"No chance." He looked horrified. "If we worked together, we'd end up killing one another. Anyway, what can I do for you?"

"You go fishing at Wash Point, don't you?"

"Yeah. I was there last weekend with Mikey. Why? Do

you want to come?"

"Me? No, thanks. I have a client whose husband went missing after going fishing there."

"Brendan Bowlings?"

"You know him?"

"Not really. Only to say 'hello' to. I heard he'd gone missing, but I assumed he'd decided to take off."

"That's what the police think. His wife says he wouldn't have left without a word. She thinks something has happened to him."

"Like what?"

"I don't know. That's what she's paying me to find out."

"He can't have fallen into the river, or someone would have found his fishing tackle on the bank."

"What's this new factory that's been built at Wash Point?"

"Your guess is as good as mine. There's no name anywhere on the building. It's a disgrace that they were ever given permission to build there. If you ask me, someone must have taken a bribe. They've fenced off a twenty metre stretch of the river. There was some good fishing in that area too. We all thought for sure that the river downstream would be polluted by whatever it is they're doing, but so far, all the tests have come back clear. It's still not right, though."

"I'll have to take a look around there at some point."

"You could always come fishing with Mikey and me."

"Thanks, but I think I'll pass on that. My life is already exciting enough, what with vacuum cleaners and caravans."

***

"Look, Jill!" Jules came bursting into my office. Mrs V was a few steps behind her. "Watch this." She was holding an anaemic-looking ball of wool. "Look what happens."

Jules put the ball of wool onto the car brochure which was on my desk. Immediately, it changed colour to match the green of the open-top sports car in the photograph.

"It's magic, isn't it?" Jules squealed with delight.

"It certainly is. Did you get one too, Mrs V?"

"I did." She held up her prized possession. "Poor Kathy is run off her feet down there. She can't serve people fast enough."

"I've no doubt Grandma will give her a bonus."

Mrs V gave me a puzzled look. "Joke?"

"What do you think?"

My two PAs couldn't wait to try out their new toy, so they returned to their desks.

"A cat could starve in here." Winky moaned.

"Sorry, I'd lost track of time." I walked over to the cupboard and opened a tin of cat food. "I'm out of salmon."

"I suppose that'll have to do, then."

I was about to put the remainder of the cat food into the fridge, when Winky coughed. "What about Lenny?"

"What about him?"

"He's hungry too."

I glanced around, but there was no sign of the ghost cat. "I can't see him."

"Surely, you know how it works by now. You can only see a ghost if he attaches himself to you. Lenny is attached to me right now."

"Of course. Sorry." I took out another bowl, filled it with cat food, and placed it next to Winky's. "There you go,

Lenny."

"Lenny says thank you."

***

I'd magicked myself over to Candlefield where I'd arranged to meet up with Maddy May who was Robbie Riddle's girlfriend. It seemed that pixies were big on alliteration when it came to names. We were meeting at Pixie Beans, a coffee shop, in Pixie Central.

In order to get inside the coffee shop, I'd been forced to shrink myself to pixie size. Maddy was wearing a charming, traditional pixie outfit complete with the cutest hat you ever did see.

"Have you and Robbie been seeing each other long, Maddy?"

"We met at high school. We've been engaged for just over a year now. We're planning to marry next year."

"Was Robbie okay on the days leading up to his disappearance?"

"Yes. He was his usual jolly self. Robbie is always happy."

"When was the last time you saw him?"

"On the morning of the day he went missing, he told me he was going to see Lionel Longfellow."

"Who's that?"

"A friend of Robbie's. Robbie has asked Lionel to be his best man." At that, Maddy began to cry. "Sorry, I just can't stand the not knowing."

"Have you spoken to Lionel?"

"Yes. He said that he and Robbie hadn't arranged to meet that day. He hadn't seen him."

"Do you think Robbie deliberately lied to you?"

"I don't want to believe that, but I can't come up with another explanation."

"Does he have any particular interests or hobbies?"

"His main interest is the human world. He's absolutely obsessed with it. He reads everything he can about it."

"Is it possible he might have gone there?"

"To the human world?" She managed a weak smile. "It's not something pixies can do. It's okay for witches, werewolves, vampires and most other sups. But pixies are six inches tall. How would we ever go unnoticed there?"

"Good point."

"A few do try, but they have to spend all of their time hidden from the view of humans. What kind of life is that?"

I promised Maddy that I would do everything I could to find her fiancé, but I wasn't overly optimistic.

Chapter 6

I would need to track down Robbie Riddle's best friend, Lionel Longfellow, but for now that would have to wait. Something was niggling at the back of my mind, and wouldn't let up. In her Will, Imelda Barrowtop had left me a journal. I hadn't been able to claim it because, in order to do so, I first had to produce Magna Mondale's book. That posed something of a problem because I had thrown the book down the Dark Well. I'd tried hard to convince myself that there wouldn't be anything in the journal that could possibly be of any interest to me. But what if there was? The only way to find out was if I could somehow recover the book from the well.

The Dark Well was on the north side of the Black Woods. It stood in a clearing between the edge of the wood and the hills beyond. The last time I'd been there, I'd had to fight off Ma Chivers. This time the area was deserted.

It was over a year since I'd disposed of the book. Unless the well was dry, the pages would have long since rotted away. Even if the well was dry, how was I going to get the book out of there? I leaned on the wall of the well, and stared down into the abyss.

"What business do you have here?" A short, plump and very ugly creature suddenly popped up from the well, causing me to stumble onto my backside.

"Who are you?" I stood up, and dusted myself down.

"I could ask you the same question."

"My name is Jill Gooder."

"I'm Timothy Troll."

"And you're a troll?"

"That's correct."

"So, you're Timothy Troll the troll?"

"Did you come here just to make fun of my name?"

I didn't, but that was certainly a fortuitous by-product. "Sorry, no. I came to try to recover my property."

"What property would that be?"

"A book. I accidentally dropped it down the well. It was over a year ago."

"A book, you say? Would it by any chance have been a very thick book containing lots of spells?"

"Yes. Have you seen it?"

He touched his forehead with his stubby little finger. "Do you see this?" He leaned forward.

"What am I supposed to be looking at?"

"This! This scar!"

I looked a little closer — there was the smallest, faintest of scars, just above his left eyebrow. "Oh, yes. I see it now."

"Your book did that. I was sitting there, minding my own business, eating cherries, when suddenly, out of the blue, a book hits me on the head. It sent me a little unnecessary for a few minutes."

"I'm terribly sorry. I had no idea that there was anyone in the well. I wouldn't have thrown it down there if I'd known."

"I thought you said it was an accident?"

Oh bum!

"Yes. An accident. That's what I meant. I didn't know there were trolls in wells. I thought they lived under bridges."

"That would be the bridge trolls."

"And you're a well troll?"

"*Well* spotted." He laughed. "*Well*? Get it?"

Don't you just hate it when you come across someone with such a puerile sense of humour?

"So? Do you have it? My book?"

"You mean the lethal weapon?"

"I've already apologised for that. Do you have it?"

"I keep all the stuff that people throw down this well."

"Is it here?"

"Of course not. If I kept it here, the well would be overflowing with rubbish. I take it home with me, and catalogue everything."

"So, you don't actually live down the well?"

"Of course not. Why would I want to live down a well? I just work here."

"I see. Can I go to your house, and collect it?"

"Hold your horses. It isn't as easy as that. I'm not running a charity, you know."

"Of course not. How much do I owe you for holding it in storage?"

"Money is no good to me."

"What do you want, then?"

"I'm a collector of fairy wings. Starlight fairy wings, to be precise."

"That's horrible and cruel. You can't go around ripping the wings off a fairy."

"Deary me. You really do not know anything about starlight fairies, do you? They shed their wings every year after they've grown a new pair. I collect the wings which they've discarded."

"Sorry. I didn't realise."

"In return for your lethal weapon of a book, I will require five pairs of starlight fairy wings."

"Okay. I'll see what I can do, but don't let anyone else

have the book in the meantime."

"I can't guarantee that. The first person to bring me five pairs of starlight fairy wings can take it."

***

This was going from the sublime to the ridiculous. To get the journal, I needed Magna Mondale's book. To get Magna Mondale's book, I now needed five pairs of starlight fairy wings.

I'd have to try to find those another day. Right now, all I wanted to do was get home, and have a quiet evening in front of the television. Custard creams, chocolate and ginger beer might also be involved.

When I got back to the house, I noticed that Blake's car was on his drive, but there was no sign of Jen's. Good! If I could snatch a quick word with him before Jen got home, I'd be able to clue him in on the blog situation.

As I walked across the road, my eardrums felt as if they might explode. The noise coming from Mr Kilbride's house was deafening. We'd all got used to his occasional bagpipe playing, and that was bad enough. But this? This was the usual cacophony multiplied by ten.

"Jill?" Blake answered the door wearing a pair of ear defenders. "Come in." He pulled them off his ears.

"What's going on next door?" I had to shout to be heard.

"I've no idea, but it's been like this for the last hour."

"I can't put up with this," I said. "I'm going around there. I'll be back in a minute."

I thumped on Kilbride's front door as hard as I could, but there was no response, so I made my way to the back of the house. Through the French doors, I could see at least five men, all dressed in kilts, and all playing the bagpipes.

I stood in front of the French doors, waving my arms around until I finally got someone's attention. Moments later, the bagpipes stopped, and it felt as though I'd gone deaf.

"Hello, Jill." Kilbride opened one of the French doors.

"We can't hear ourselves think, out here, Mr Kilbride."

"I'm so sorry. When the boys and I get together and start jamming, we can sometimes get a little carried away."

Boys? Jamming?

"You have to dial down the volume."

"We were just about to call it a day, anyway. We need to conserve our energy for the big day."

"What 'big day' would that be?"

"The first ever Washbridge Bagpipe Festival is being held in two days' time. There'll be hundreds of pipers on the streets. It's going to be spectacular."

"It sounds unmissable."

"That's better." Blake sighed. "What was going on?"

"There's a gaggle of bagpipers next door. They're all here for a bagpipe festival in Washbridge."

"I must remember to give that a wide berth."

"You and me both. Look, Blake, the reason I'm here is that I'm worried about Jen. I think she might get you into trouble with the rogue retrievers."

"What has she been saying, this time?"

"My sister told me about something called the Wizard's Wife's blog. After looking at it, I'm almost certain that Jen must be behind it. Take a look at it yourself—it's easy to find. See what you think. If it is Jen, then you need to get her to stop, and delete what she's already done."

"I will. And you can say it. I wouldn't blame you."

"Say what?"

"That you told me so. You said it was a bad idea for me to come clean with Jen."

"It's too late to worry about that now. That particular horse has already bolted. Just make sure you get the blog shut down as soon as you can."

"Will do. Thanks again, Jill."

***

As I was on my way back to the house, Megan Lovemore pulled onto her driveway.

"Hi, Megan."

"Oh, hi, Jill." She seemed strangely subdued, and barely managed a smile.

"Are you okay?"

"Yeah. I think I could be coming down with a cold, though."

That might explain the unusual attire. Megan usually favoured T-shirts and shorts, but today she was wearing jeans with a polo neck top.

"I hope you feel better soon."

The house was looking spotless. Our new cleaner, Agatha Crustie, had been around earlier in the day. It still stuck in my craw that I was paying someone else to use magic to clean the house when I could have done that myself, at no cost. But how would I ever have explained it away to Jack?

My phone rang. It was Kathy.

"What a day I've had." She sounded exhausted.

"I hear the Chameleon Wool launch was a success."

"That's an understatement. We've taken a small fortune today, and I'm absolutely shattered."

"Just think about the bonus that Grandma will be giving you."

"Fat chance of that. The reason I called was because I wanted to tell you about Lizzie."

"Is she okay?"

"She's great. You remember I told you about the 'best friend' essay?"

"Did you manage to persuade her to write about another one of her friends?"

"No, but as it turned out, I needn't have worried. Everyone loved her story. The teacher gave her full marks, and said her writing showed an active imagination. Better still, all the kids want to be her friend now. They all want to know more about Caroline."

"That's great, Kathy. I'm so pleased for her. Give her a 'well done' kiss from me."

"Will do. Now, I'm going to go upstairs to sleep for a week."

Jack arrived home just in time for us to have dinner together.

"How's the fish and chip case coming along?" I grinned.

"No more of your stupid puns, please. I had enough of those this morning."

"Okay. I'll *fry* my best." I broke down in tears of laughter.

Jack huffed and puffed, and then went upstairs to get changed. When I'd eventually managed to compose myself, I went to find him.

"Have you done with all the fish jokes?" he asked.

"Yes. No more, I promise."

"If you must know, I've been taken off the fish and chip case. I spent most of the day trying to help my colleagues at Washbridge police station."

"Leo Riley?"

"No, thank goodness. One of the detectives I used to work with asked me to check West Chippings' missing persons file. It seems that there are three unidentified coma victims in Washbridge Hospital. They thought one of them might be on our missing persons list."

"Were they?"

"No. I checked their photographs against our files, and there were no matches."

"Isn't that kind of weird? Three unidentified coma victims, I mean?"

"Very. According to Tom, the guy I was trying to help, the patients were admitted over a period of three months. No one knows what happened to them, or even who they are. It appears that all three were found collapsed in the street."

"What are you going to do about it?"

"We? As in West Chipping? We won't be doing anything. It isn't our case. I don't suppose there's much the Washbridge guys can do either, unless they find a match on a missing persons list somewhere else in the country. Their only other hope is that the patients regain consciousness."

"I have some news, too. Mrs Rollo is moving out."

"Why?"

"She said that she wants to live next-door to someone who will appreciate her baking."

"She'll be searching for a long time, then. Are you serious? Is she really leaving?"

"Yeah. She's going to Australia with Marco for six months at least. She's going to rent out the house."

"I have some big news too."

"It doesn't relate to caravans, does it?"

"It's my parents' golden wedding anniversary next week, and we're all invited to the party."

"All?"

"You, me, Kathy, Peter and the kids, plus all of your birth family."

"Next week? It's a bit short notice, isn't it?"

"Mum had insisted she didn't want a big do, but then she changed her mind at the last minute. It'll be great, won't it?"

"Great, yeah."

Oh bum!

Chapter 7

The next morning, Jack was still super excited about the golden wedding anniversary party.

"I can't wait for you to meet my parents."

"Me neither."

To be fair, that meeting was long overdue. Jack and I had been together for well over a year. It wasn't like we hadn't been invited up there before, but each time there had been some reason why I wasn't able to make it. This time, there could be no excuses. You only got to celebrate your golden wedding once, and Jack would never forgive me if I tried to wheedle my way out of it. My main concern was that my birth family were also invited. Aunt Lucy, Lester and the twins should be okay, but what about Grandma?

"You are going to invite your birth family, aren't you?" Jack must have been reading my mind. "Mum will be disappointed if they don't all come."

"Of course."

"Promise?"

"I promise."

He glanced at my hands.

"What?"

"I was just checking you didn't have your fingers crossed."

"It's nice to know you trust me."

Just then, there was a knock at the door.

"I'll get it." I volunteered. Anything to escape the third degree.

It was Mrs Rollo; she was holding a cakebox.

"I'm sorry to call around so early, Jill, but my taxi will be here in a few minutes."

"You're leaving already?"

"Yes. I'm booked on the early train."

"Come in." I led the way through to the kitchen. "Jack, Mrs Rollo has come to say goodbye."

"We're both sorry to see you leave," Jack said.

"I'm sorry to go. You two have been wonderful neighbours."

"Let me take that," I offered.

"I wanted to bake you a 'farewell' cake." She passed me the box. "I hope you enjoy it."

"I'm sure we will," Jack said. "We've enjoyed everything you've baked for us."

He was such an accomplished liar.

"Take care you two." She gave each of us a hug. "The letting agent tells me that they've already rented out my house. You should have new neighbours in the next few days. Anyway, I'd better run, or I'll miss my train."

We saw her to the door, and waved her off.

"I'll miss her," Jack said, after she'd gone.

"We've enjoyed everything you've baked for us." I mocked. "You're such a hypocrite."

"I was just being nice."

"I'll go and throw this in the bin, shall I?" I picked up the box.

"Wait! You can't do that. It's her 'farewell' cake."

"It will be farewell for us, if we eat it."

"We should at least try one piece each. What harm can it do?"

"You eat the first slice. If you survive, then I'll have some."

"Okay. We'll eat it tonight after dinner."

"Are you sure? Don't you even want to take a look at it

before committing?" I reached for the box lid.

"No." Jack grabbed my hand. "Let's not look until we're ready to eat it."

That sounded like a dangerously insane strategy.

***

All of the bottle tops had been removed from the windows of the toll booth. Mr Ivers wasn't on duty today; it was an older man with a tattoo of a stapler on his forehead.

"Morning." I handed over the payment. "What happened to the bottle tops?"

"I took them down. I couldn't see a thing through the windows. And if that nutter, Ivers, puts them back up, he'll have me to answer to."

"Right." And then curiosity got the better of me. "Can I ask, why do you have a tattoo of a stapler on your forehead?"

"The tattoo artist couldn't draw a hole punch."

Huh? "I see. Okay, thanks."

I drove past Ever on my way into the office. There was already a long queue outside, waiting for the shop to open. It looked as though Kathy had another busy day ahead of her, as Chameleon Wool continued to sell like hot cakes. Maybe I should try to come up with some magic-based product that I could sell to humans. It had to be more lucrative than the P.I. business. But if I did, what were the chances that I'd get away with it like Grandma? Slim to none, I'd wager. In fact, I wouldn't put it past Grandma to dob me into the rogue retrievers.

It was Jules' day off, so Mrs V had both desks to herself.

"I thought I'd sit at this one in the morning," she said. "It gets the sun. Then, this afternoon, I'll move to that one."

"I can see you've given this some serious thought. Are you and Jules okay together now?"

"Yes, it's going to work just fine. It's nice to have someone to discuss yarn projects with. I had hoped that *you* might develop an interest, but that's never going to happen, is it?"

"Sorry to be such a disappointment. I see you're using the Chameleon Wool."

"Yes." Mrs V held up the multi-coloured scarf she was knitting. "It makes life so much easier. I just have to be careful that I don't have any colour mishaps."

"How do you mean?"

"I was half way through the red section when I must have nudged the ball of wool, which came to rest against my green handbag. I'd knitted three rows of emerald green before I realised what had happened."

"I can see how that could be problematic."

"Apparently, if you squeeze the ball of wool very hard, it's meant to 'lock' the current colour so it won't inadvertently change, but I don't seem to have the knack."

"You should report it to Kathy. It sounds like a design flaw to me."

Kathy was going to love me for that. Snigger.

Winky had his head stuck inside another brochure. At first, I assumed he was drooling over cars again, but it turned out that this one was for luxury watches.

"Which one do you prefer?" He pointed to three different timepieces.

"Have you seen the prices?" I couldn't believe my eyes.

"Money is no object."

"You don't still believe that you're going to win the lottery, do you?"

"I don't *believe*. I *know*."

"Have you been consulting Madam Winkesca?"

"Let's just say that I had a premonition."

Poor, deluded fool. He was going to be so disappointed.

I had planned to visit Wash Point, to take a look at the stretch of river where Brendan Bowlings usually fished, but it had started to rain, and I didn't fancy the prospect of trudging through mud in my heels.

Mrs V walked into my office, and closed the door behind her. "Jill, did you hear about the man who died in the industrial freezer?"

"I saw the article in The Bugle."

"The man's widow is here. She'd like to see you."

"What's her name?"

"Mrs Rice."

"Ice? How very unfortunate, given what happened to—"

"Not Ice. Rrrrrice." Mrs V Made a point of rolling the 'R'.

"Oh, right, okay. You'd better show her in."

"She's very upset, so I told her to take two scarves."

"Very considerate."

"Do have a seat, Mrs Rice. My condolences on your loss."

"Thank you. Please call me Amy." Her mascara had run down her right cheek, but I felt it best not to mention it.

"How can I help you, today?"

"I want you to find my husband's murderer."

"I understood that his death had been a tragic accident."

"That's exactly what they want you to think."

"They?"

"Whoever murdered him, of course."

"If you believe it was murder, you really should be talking to the police."

"Don't you think I already have? I spoke to some chap named Riley. The man is a waste of space. He insists that Douglas' death was an accident."

"But you don't believe that?"

"I know it wasn't. Douglas was the most cautious man I've ever known. He used to drive me crazy. He always double and triple checked every door was locked. He checked the tyre pressures on his car every other day. He would never cross a road unless the light was on green — even if there wasn't a car to be seen for miles. He took zero risks — particularly when it came to his work."

"Accidents can happen even to the most careful of us."

"Not to Douglas. This was foul play, and I want you to find out what really happened. How much will it cost me?"

I told her my daily rate, and she didn't so much as blink.

"That's fine."

"Plus expenses, and I do ask for a small retainer."

"That's okay. How quickly can you get started?"

"Pretty much straight away."

"Excellent."

Amy Rice filled me in with details of the small cold storage business that was owned and run by her husband, and his twin brothers, Gordon and Jordan.

"Would you like a photograph of Doug?"

"Yes please."

She took out her phone. "This is the most recent photo I

have; Doug is the one in the centre. I took it on the day the brothers celebrated that the business had been running for forty years—it was started by their father."

The photograph had been taken in front of Rice Cold Storage.

"His brothers really are identical, aren't they?"

"Yes. Gordon is the one in T-shirt and jeans. Doug wasn't very thrilled when Gordon turned up wearing those. He wanted them all to wear suits for the photo, which he intended to give to The Bugle. He thought the story would give them a bit of free publicity."

"Did they fall out about that?"

"Not really. Doug was annoyed, but not surprised. Gordon never wears anything else. It doesn't matter whether he's at work or going out for the evening. It's always a black T-shirt and blue jeans."

"Could you let me have a copy of this photo?"

"Yes. I'll email it to you."

We talked for a few more minutes, and I promised I'd get back to her as soon as I'd finished my initial investigations.

"Me too," Winky said, once Amy Rice had left.

"You too, what?"

"I wasn't talking to you. I was just telling Lenny that I'm hungry, too."

"I suppose that means you want me to feed you?"

"Do you have salmon?" He knew that I did because he'd seen me bring some in earlier that morning.

"I do. Is that for both of you?"

Winky turned to his left. "Salmon, Lenny?" He grinned. "Obviously." Then he turned back to me. "Lenny would like salmon too. Red, not pink."

This was starting to get expensive. It was bad enough having to buy salmon for Winky, but now I was shelling out for his ghost friend, too. It was a good thing I had a few paying cases. I'd need the money they generated just to keep pace with the salmon bill.

**

I wanted to talk to Kathy about the golden wedding anniversary party, so I nipped down to Ever. I should have known better—the shop was still chock-a-block with people wanting to buy the new Chameleon Wool. Kathy and Chloe were run off their feet behind the counter; there was no way I was going to get to talk to her.

"Have you decided to buy some Chameleon Wool?" Grandma had sneaked up behind me. She was wearing a bathing costume and purple sun-glasses, and had obviously just come down from the sun terrace.

"You made me jump. No, I just wanted a quick word with Kathy."

"That's not possible. Can't you see she's run off her feet?"

"It looks as though they both are. Why don't you give them a hand?"

"Me?" She cackled at the idea. "I'm management. I'm too busy strategizing to be customer-facing."

"On the roof terrace? In your bathing costume?"

"You're getting in the way. If you aren't here to make a purchase, I'm going to have to ask you to leave."

"Will you tell Kathy I came in, and ask her to give me a call?"

"If I remember."

I fought my way back out of the shop, and took a deep breath.

That woman drove me crazy!

After that encounter, I needed a coffee and a blueberry muffin, so I popped my head in the door of Coffee Triangle, just to make sure that the giant triangles had all been removed. Only when I was sure that the coast was clear, did I venture inside.

What? Of course I wasn't *afraid* of the giant triangles. They just took up a lot of room.

As I munched on the deliciousness that was the blueberry muffin, my mind wandered to the anniversary party. Could I really unleash Grandma on Jack's parents? The prospect terrified me, but I could think of no way around it.

"Jill?" A tall, slim woman with red, frizzy hair was standing next to my table. She was wearing a pinafore dress covered in a pattern made up of tiny lollipops. "It is you, isn't it?"

"I'm Jill Gooder."

"I knew it was you. You haven't changed a bit."

I had zero idea who the woman with the squeaky, high-pitched voice was.

"Sorry, I—err—"

"It's Lolly."

"Lolly?" And then the penny dropped—with a ginormous clang. "Lolly Jolly?"

"That's right. It's so lovely to see you again." She reached down and gave me a big hug.

Lolly Jolly had been our next-door neighbour when we were kids. Kathy and I used to do our best to avoid her because she was so annoying. I hadn't seen her in years.

"I didn't realise you still lived around here, Lolly."

"I've lived in London for the last ten years, but I've just moved back."

"I'd love to stop and chat, but there's somewhere I have to be." I stood up.

"What about your muffin?"

"I'm not as hungry as I thought. Anyway, lovely to see you."

"Does Kathy still live in Washbridge?"

"Yes. She's married now with two kids."

"What about you?"

"I'm with someone, too."

"Kids?"

"Me? No." I checked my watch. "Sorry, I must rush."

"Okay. Nice to see you again, Jill. I'll make sure to look you and Kathy up."

Great!

Chapter 8

On the day that Robbie Riddle had gone missing, he'd told his fiancée that he was meeting Lionel Longfellow. I'd arranged to meet with Lionel at Pixie Beans—the same coffee shop where I'd spoken with Maddy May. Once again, I'd had to shrink myself in order to get inside.

"I understand that you and Robbie were good friends?"

"Best friends, I'd say. I've known Robbie since I was a kid. Did you know that he'd asked me to be his best man?"

"Yeah, Maddy mentioned it. I assume you know that Robbie told Maddy that he was meeting you on the day he disappeared?"

"Yes, but I can't think why he said that."

"If you're covering for him, now would be a good time to tell me."

"I'm not! I honestly have no idea why he would have told her that."

"Presumably, because he didn't want Maddy to know what he was really doing, or where he was going."

"I suppose so."

"And you have no idea where that might have been?"

"I honestly don't have a clue. Look, Robbie and I are great friends, but to be completely honest with you, he isn't the most exciting pixie in the world. He's only interested in three things: Maddy, PixieBall and the human world."

"What's PixieBall?"

"Think soccer, but on a much smaller scale."

"Maddy did mention his interest in the human world."

"I'm not surprised. He's always banging on about it. I don't see the attraction myself, but Robbie is completely obsessed. He reads and watches everything he can find about it. He really envies the full-sized sups who can travel back and forth between here and the human world without any problems."

"Do you think it's possible he might have gone there?"

"No way. Robbie would have loved to, but he isn't stupid enough to run that risk. How long do you think a six-inch tall pixie would last there before someone noticed? I don't know where he is, but I'm pretty sure you can rule out the human world."

***

In order to escape Lolly Jolly, I'd been forced to abandon my muffin in Coffee Triangle, so I felt entitled to take a muffin-break in Cuppy C.

"A cup of tea and one of your finest blueberry muffins please, Pearl."

"Would that be a mini muffin?"

"What do you think?" I glanced around the shop. "Where's Amber?"

"I can't tell you. It's top secret."

"Now, I really want to know. Come on, you can tell me."

"Okay, but we don't want this to get out until we're ready to launch. You know what Miles Best is like. He'll steal our idea."

"Please tell me you two haven't come up with another hare-brained scheme. I thought you'd agreed that you should focus on the core services, and not keep getting distracted."

"We're not changing anything here in the shop, I promise. Are you sure you want to see?"

"Definitely."

Pearl called one of her assistants over from the cake shop and then led me to the back door.

"Just wait there, Jill. I won't be a minute." She slipped out of the door.

What on earth were the twins up to this time? Despite Pearl's words of reassurance, I wasn't optimistic.

"You can come outside now, Jill." Pearl's voice sounded slightly muffled.

I stepped out into the narrow alleyway that ran behind the shop. Standing in front of me were two figures dressed in leathers — one yellow and the other pink. They were both wearing crash helmets with the visors down. Next to them, was a pair of motor scooters — again one yellow, the other pink.

"What do you think?" the yellow biker said. She sounded an awful lot like Amber.

"I like the colours, but what's this all about?"

"Deliveries, of course," Pearl, the pink biker, said.

"You're going to start a delivery service for Cuppy C?"

"Come on, Jill." Amber raised the visor on her helmet. "Even you have to admit that this is pure genius."

"No other tea room or cake shop offers this service." Pearl removed her helmet, and ran her fingers through her hair.

"Did it ever occur to either of you that there might be a reason for that?"

"It's because no one else has our vision," Amber said, proudly.

"Yeah." Pearl nodded. "We're breaking new ground."

"Or, just maybe—" I glanced again at the scooters. "Everyone else has realised that it's not cost-effective to offer a delivery service for a tea room. Or a cake shop."

"Rubbish! People will love it." Pearl opened the lid of the plastic box which was directly behind the seat. "We've had special takeaway menus printed." She handed me one of the tri-folds.

"Cuppy C U Soon?"

"Catchy, isn't it?" Amber said. "I thought of that."

I studied the menu. "The prices are exactly the same as in the shop."

"That's only fair," Pearl said. "We didn't think it was right to charge more."

"I assume you'll levy a separate delivery charge?"

"We can't do that." Amber shook her head. "That wouldn't be fair either."

"I don't see any mention of a minimum order on here."

"That's because there isn't one."

"What if someone orders a single cup of tea, or just one cupcake?"

"No one is going to do that." Pearl sounded exasperated at my questioning.

"Yeah," Amber said. "We're going to open up a whole new market with this venture. We'll probably double our takings."

"What do you think, Jill?" Pearl asked. "Be honest."

Although she'd said I should be honest, I knew the twins well enough to know that's not what they really wanted. They wanted me to tell them that I thought it was a brilliant idea, but I had my integrity to think of. I wasn't going to say something if I didn't mean it.

"I think it's great. I'm sure it will do really well."

What? Who are you calling a hypocrite?

***

Back at my office, Mrs V was still engrossed in her knitting.

"Any messages, Mrs V?"

"Nothing for you, but Jules did call with some news."

"Oh?"

"Apparently, that young man of hers—what's his name?"

"Gilbert."

"Of course. He's got himself a new job. Jules sounded delighted."

"That's great news. What will he be doing?"

"She did tell me, but I didn't really understand it. Something about testing soft hair, I think."

"Soft hair?"

"That's what she said."

"Whatever it is, it must be better than peddling that awful Magical Skincare."

"Winky! What's going on?"

He was sitting on the sofa. In front of him, snaking across my office, was a line of cats.

He obviously hadn't heard me, so I started towards the sofa.

"Hey, you!" A Siamese cat called out. "There's a queue here, in case you hadn't noticed."

"Sorry, I just need a word with Winky."

"Next!" Winky said, without looking up.

"What's going on here?" I demanded.

"You're holding up the queue."

"And I'll keep holding it up until I know what this is all about."

"They're here to sign up for a subscription to Moonlight Gym. Now, if you wouldn't mind?"

"I do mind, actually. I mind very much. I told you that you can't use my office as a gym."

"And I told you that I have no intention of doing that. You have my solemn word that I won't be using this office."

"I'm supposed to take your word for that, am I?"

"If I'm lying, then you need never buy me salmon again."

"Oh?" That took me by surprise. There was no way Winky would make that promise unless he was actually telling the truth. Maybe he was renting premises elsewhere?

"Come on, lady!" A Persian cat yelled. "Get out of the way!"

While Winky was processing all the membership subscriptions, I busied myself researching the death at Rice Brothers. The cold storage business had been founded in the 1970s by Ronald Rice. After his death, the business had passed to his three sons: Douglas, Gordon and Jordan. Douglas Rice had been found dead in the freezer by his brother Gordon. According to the news articles I'd read, it had apparently been a tragic accident. It seemed that Douglas had fallen, banged his head, rendering himself unconscious, and had frozen to death. Amy Rice, however, was adamant that this had been no accident.

I would need to take a look around the cold storage unit, and speak to the other two brothers.

My phone rang.
"Kathy?"

"Your grandmother said you called in to see me?"

"I'm amazed she passed the message on. Are you on a break?"

"No. I finished an hour early."

"Grandma said you could go early?"

"I've barely stopped all day, but things started to slow down about half an hour ago, so I told her that unless she let me finish early today, she wouldn't see me tomorrow."

"That was brave of you."

"I know, but it worked. What was it you wanted?"

"Are you on your way home?"

"I'm already back."

"I've had enough for today, too. Why don't I pop over there now?"

"Okay. I'll get the kettle on."

"And break out the custard creams. Preferably not soggy ones, this time."

I'd no sooner finished on the call than the room suddenly became colder, and I could sense a ghost was about to appear. Could it be Lenny again? Probably not because he was so small that he didn't usually have a noticeable effect on the temperature.

"Colonel? Nice to see you. Where's Priscilla?"

"Visiting her sister. She recently passed over, so Cilla is showing her the ropes."

"I was actually just on my way out."

"Sorry. This won't take a minute. I have problems with the house again, I'm afraid."

"What's Murray Murray up to now?"

"Nothing. The new owner is a delight. He hasn't given us a moment's trouble since you carried out the 'exorcism'."

"What's wrong, then?"

"We have ghost problems."

Huh? "Sorry, I don't follow."

"Another ghost has moved in. Without being invited, I might add."

"Is it someone you know?"

"No. The bounder just turned up out of the blue. He seems to think that it's acceptable to steal valuables from the house, and take them back to Ghost Town."

"I didn't know that was possible."

"Me neither, but he seems to have found a way to do it."

"What's he doing with the stuff he's stolen?"

"I don't know. I assume he will sell it. The problem is that the new owner has noticed that a few things have gone missing, and I can tell he's getting frustrated by it. I get the impression he's having second thoughts about the house."

"Do you think he might sell?"

"That's the worry. I'm concerned that if he does, that same property developer might show an interest again."

"I have to confess that I'm not too well up on ghost theft from the human world, but I have a friend who might be able to help. I'll speak to her."

"Thanks, Jill. Once again, I'm indebted to you."

After the colonel had disappeared, I called Mad to ask if she had any advice on how to handle his situation, but there was no answer, so I left a message on her voicemail.

When I went through to the outer office, Jules had popped in, with Gilbert.

"Hello, young man. I hear you've got a new job, testing hair."

Both he and Jules gave me a puzzled look.

"I'm going to be working as a software tester," he said.

I glanced at Mrs V who just shrugged.

"Of course, that makes much more sense." I turned to Jules. "What brings you in on your day off? Can't you stay away?"

"Last night, I worked out how to get Chameleon Wool to 'lock' on a colour. As we were in town anyway, I thought I'd drop in and show Annabel."

"Watch, Jill." Mrs V picked up the ball of Chameleon Wool, pressed her thumb into the centre, and then tapped it on the desk. "See, it's locked." To prove it, she placed it against her red top. This time the ball of wool did not change colour. "And then you do the same thing to unlock it."

"You should buy some of this wool, Jill," Jules said. "It's the best thing since sliced bread."

I considered putting her right on that particular claim, but my thoughts on that subject had already fallen on stony ground, so I let it pass.

Chapter 9

Kathy had a cup of tea waiting for me when I arrived at her place, but she didn't have any custard creams.

"Why not?"

"I haven't had the time to buy any more, and you said you didn't like the soft ones, so I threw them out."

"You did what? A soggy custard cream is better than no custard cream at all."

"They're still in the bin, if you want to dig them out."

"Don't be disgusting."

What? Yes, alright, I admit it—I did consider it.

"The Chameleon Wool seems to be a success," I said, once we'd made ourselves comfortable in the lounge. "Mrs V and Jules think it's—"

"The best thing since sliced bread?"

"I was going to say that they think it's great."

"Everyone does. Your grandmother might be a pain in the rear, but her inventions are incredible. I don't know how she does it."

"I do," I said, under my breath, and then out loud I said, "It's a mystery."

"What was it you wanted to talk to me about?"

"It's Jack's parents' golden wedding anniversary next weekend, and they're having a party."

"You still haven't met them yet, have you?"

"No. I've always been too busy."

"You can't duck out of this one."

"I know. I've already said that I'll go, but the invitation extends to all my family."

"Including us?"

"Last time I checked, you were my family."

"Great. I'll ask Pete's Mum to have the kids."

"They're invited too."

"I want to be able to let my hair down. I can't do that if I've got to keep an eye on the kids. I'll get Pete's Mum to take them to Bug World. They've been bugging me forever to take them there. *Bugging*? Get it?"

"Hey, I'm the comedian in this family."

"I can't say I've noticed." She drank the last of her tea. "I'll have to buy a new outfit, obviously. We could go shopping together."

"No, thanks. This thing is going to be painful enough as it is, without having to endure a shopping trip with you."

"Please yourself. I'll get Pete to come with me."

"I don't know what to do about Grandma."

"How do you mean?"

"She's been invited too. She's my family, remember?"

Kathy's face fell. "I hadn't thought of that."

"I've thought about nothing else."

"You could always *forget* to tell her."

"Oh, yeah. Because that would work. You know Grandma. She doesn't miss a thing. I'll have to invite her. My only hope is that I can paint a picture so bleak, she won't want to come."

"How are you going to do that?"

"I could say that Jack's parents are teetotal. That might put her off."

"Good idea. It's worth a try. What about your Aunt Lucy, and the twins?"

"They're invited too. In fact, I'm going to talk to Aunt Lucy, to see what she thinks about Grandma going to the party."

"Well, even if your grandmother does go, you can still

count Pete and me in. It's been ages since I went to a party."

"Just don't show me up."

"When did I ever?"

Before I could list all such occasions, my phone rang. It was Mad, returning my call.

"You rang?"

"Yeah. I need your advice."

"Fire away."

"I'm at Kathy's, at the moment."

"Can't talk? No problem. How about we meet at the library later—after it's closed? I thought we could make a start on your training, and you can tell me what you need advice on."

"Tonight? I guess so. What time?"

"Seven o' clock?"

"Okay. See you then."

"What was that all about?" Kathy asked, after I'd finished on the call.

"Nothing. Just a case I'm working on. Hey, you'll never guess who I bumped into in Coffee Triangle."

"Murray Murray?"

"No. I doubt he slums it in Coffee Triangle. I bumped into Lolly Jolly."

"Lolly? I haven't seen her for years—thank goodness. Has she changed? She must have."

"No. She's pretty much the same—just taller. Same squeaky voice, same frizzy hair, and same bad dress sense. She was wearing a pinafore dress covered in little lollipops."

"Wow! What did she have to say?"

"Not much. Just that she's been living in London for the last ten years, but now she's moved back up here. She asked about you."

"I hope you told her that I'd emigrated."

"Actually, I gave her your phone number, and said you'd love it if she got in touch."

***

Even though I'd only just had a cup of tea at Kathy's, I didn't refuse another at Aunt Lucy's. And, more importantly, Aunt Lucy had custard creams — of the non-soggy variety.

"Have you seen the twins' scooters?" I said, as we took a seat at the kitchen table.

"I have, and I'm not very happy about them. Those two were never very confident on bicycles when they were kids. I'm scared they'll fall off and hurt themselves. Can't you talk some sense into them, Jill?"

"It would be a waste of time even trying because they don't listen to me. I reckon they'll lose money hand over fist, so I don't think it will last for long."

"I hope you're right."

"The main reason I came over was to tell you that you've been invited to Jack's parents' golden wedding anniversary party. It's next weekend. Can you and Lester make it at such short notice?"

"Just try stopping us. It will be lovely to meet Jack's family."

"Kathy and Peter are going, and I still need to ask the twins. I was going to do it yesterday, but then they told me about the new delivery service, and I completely forgot."

"They'll definitely be up for it, but I'm not sure about Alan and William. They work such odd hours. What about

Grandma?"

"I wanted to ask you about that. I know I have to tell her, but I'd really rather she didn't go. You know what she's like. I'd be on tenterhooks all the time. I'm hoping to convince her that she wouldn't enjoy it."

"How do you plan to do that?"

"I thought I could tell her that Jack's parents are both teetotal."

"That might work. It's worth a try." Aunt Lucy picked up the biscuit tin. "Another?"

"Go on then."

What? It would have been rude to refuse.

"Aunt Lucy, there is something else I wanted to ask you. Do you happen to know where I could get hold of starlight fairy wings? The ones they've discarded, obviously."

"Why do you need those?"

"It's a long story. Do you remember Magna Mondale's book?"

"The one you got from the sealed room? Of course I do."

"I had to throw it down the Dark Well."

"Grandma told me."

"Now I need it back, and it turns out the well is guarded by a troll. He'll only let me have the book if I can get him five pairs of starlight fairy wings."

"I see. I do know that they're very much sought after. There are a lot of collectors. I can make a few phone calls, if you like?"

"That would be great." I stood up. "I'd better get back."

"Okay. Good luck with Grandma."

***

It was my turn to make dinner.

"What's this?" Jack poked at the brown lump on his plate.

"Steak and kidney pie."

"What's this brown wafer thing?"

"That's the gravy."

"Really?" He picked up the 'wafer' and broke it in half.

"Just eat it and stop complaining. I've told you before that it would be better if you did the cooking every day."

"Better for you, you mean."

"I would do the washing up."

"By *washing up*, do you mean stack the dirty dishes in the dishwasher?"

"It isn't as easy as you make it out to be. There's a certain knack to it."

"If you say so. Did you check with everyone about the anniversary party?"

"Kathy and Peter are coming, but they're going to leave the kids with Peter's Mum."

"Why? The kids are welcome to come."

"I know, but Kathy said she wanted a break from them."

"What about the others?"

"Aunt Lucy and Lester are a definite *yes*. I'm pretty sure the twins will be coming, but I don't know about their husbands."

"What about your grandmother?"

"What about her?"

"Is she coming?"

"I don't know. I haven't managed to catch up with her yet."

"You have to try. I promised I'd let Mum know the numbers in a day or so."

"Okay. Will do." I checked my watch. "I have to nip out for a while."

"Where?"

"I'm meeting Mad at the library."

"Doesn't it close at seven?"

"Yeah, but she works there, remember? She's helping me with some research on a case I'm working on."

"Which case?"

"Nothing you'd be interested in." I grabbed my bag.

"What about your slice of Mrs Rollo's cake?"

"You promised to have the first piece, remember? If you haven't died from food poisoning when I get back, I'll have some. See you later."

***

Mad was watching for me, through the window.

"Before we start the training," I said. "I had a visit from the colonel earlier. He's having problems with a ghost who is stealing valuables from his old house. He's worried that the current owner may get fed up and sell the house to a property developer. Is there anything you can do to help?"

"Possibly. Can you ask him to put together a full description of the items that have been taken? Photos would be great if he happens to have any."

"Okay. I'll get the colonel on it. Now, how are we going to do this thing?"

"Good question. I've been racking my brain, and I still don't know where to start. I can move between this world and Ghost Town effortlessly, but I have no idea how I do it. It's a bit like breathing—I just do it."

"We can only do our best. If it doesn't work, then we'll

just have to tell Aubrey it isn't happening. Why don't you transport yourself over there now? I'll apply all my powers of focus on you, and see what I can pick up."

"Okay. Ready?"

"On three. One, two, three."

Mad disappeared, but despite giving it maximum focus, I didn't pick up anything I could lock in on.

"Any good?" Mad reappeared.

"No. I didn't get anything. Try again, but this time when you're in GT, shout my name."

"What good will that do?"

"Probably none, but we have nothing to lose by trying."

"Okay."

"Three, two, one."

I turned my focus onto the space where Mad had been standing, but I sensed nothing. Absolutely nothing.

Then, I heard something. A voice. It was Mad. And I could hear her calling my name.

I had to try to forget that she was in Ghost Town, and just focus on her voice. If I could magic myself towards it, then maybe — just maybe.

My head was throbbing with the effort of focussing so hard, but I could feel it was starting to work. It was the same sensation I felt when I magicked myself between Candlefield and Washbridge.

I hit the ground with a thump. Where was I? The images swimming before my eyes had no real definition. It was as though they were melting and blending into one another. Then, without warning, I landed with a thud again. I felt as though all of the breath had been punched out of me.

I was back in the library.

"Are you okay?" Mad helped me to my feet.

"I think so."

"Where did you go?"

"I don't know, but I don't think it was Ghost Town."

"Could you hear me shouting your name?"

"Yes. I tried to follow your voice, but I'm not sure it worked."

"Do you want to give it another try?"

"I can't. I'm beat. I feel like I've been put through the wringer."

"Shall I tell Aubrey it's a non-starter?"

"Not yet."

Chapter 10

Jack had just showered. I was still lazing in bed.

"I'd like to let my mum have the final numbers tonight, if I can," he said.

"Don't worry. I'm on it. Did I hear you say you were going to make a fry-up, this morning?"

"I never mentioned a fry-up."

"I could have sworn you did. I really fancy one."

"You know where the frying pan is."

"If you really loved me, you'd make me a fry-up."

"If *you* really loved *me*, you wouldn't resort to blackmail tactics." He grinned. "Anyway, don't forget you have Mrs Rollo's cake to eat."

"Did you try a slice?"

"Yes. It was surprisingly nice."

"Liar."

"It was, honestly. I think she must have made a special effort because it was the last one she'd be baking for us." He bent over and gave me a kiss.

"Why don't you come back to bed?"

"I'd love to, but I have a meeting with the boss at eight-thirty."

"*I'm* your boss."

"Bye, Jill."

By the time I'd showered, dressed, and dragged myself downstairs, there wasn't time to make a cooked breakfast, even if I could have been bothered to do it, so I settled for cornflakes. Jack had apparently survived the night after eating a slice of Mrs Rollo's cake, so I thought that maybe I'd take some to work for me, Mrs V and Jules. I was just about to cut three slices when a sudden thought stopped me in my tracks.

I checked the kitchen bin; it was empty, so I slipped on some shoes, went outside, and checked the dustbin.

"I'll kill him!"

There, on top of the rubbish, was a slice of cake, minus one bite. Jack must have tried it, and then thrown the rest away. Just wait until I got my hands on him!

When I left the house, Megan was just coming out of her front door. She was wearing a silk scarf around her neck—something I'd never seen her do before.

"Megan! Hi."

"Morning, Jill." She still didn't seem her usual bubbly self.

"Are you okay? You seem a little subdued."

"I'm fine." Her forced smile was far from convincing. "I have a bit of a cold, that's all."

"Are you sure?"

"Yes, positive. I have to get going."

"Okay. Bye."

That's when I spotted it. On her neck, not quite hidden by the scarf, was a small bruise. There were any number of ways that might have happened, but my mind went back to what she'd told me about signing up with Love Bites, the dating agency which matched vampires with humans.

I had bad vibes.

***

Despite the fact that Jack had tried to poison me with Mrs Rollo's cake, I still had to get him the final numbers for the golden wedding anniversary party.

First stop—Cuppy C.

"Hi, girls. How is the takeaway service going?"

"It starts tomorrow," Amber said. "We've already had a lot of interest."

"That's great. The reason I'm here is it's Jack's parents' golden wedding anniversary next weekend, and you're invited to the party. Alan and William too."

"A party?" Amber beamed. "Count me in. William won't be able to make it though. He has to work."

"Count me in, too," Pearl said. "But Alan will be working."

"Do you ever go out with your husbands?"

"Not if we can help it," Amber said, and they both laughed.

"Okay. That's you two and Aunt Lucy, so far. I just have to check with Grandma."

"Grandma?" Pearl looked horrified.

"You didn't tell us she was going." Amber's smile had dissolved.

"I'm hoping she won't, but I have to at least ask her."

"Grandma is never going to say 'no' to a party," Pearl said.

"She might when I tell her that Jack's parents are teetotal."

"Are they?"

"Of course not."

"How very sly of you." Amber nodded in approval. "That's a brilliant idea."

Just then, Daze and Blaze walked into the shop.

"Will you join us, Jill?" Daze called.

"I haven't ordered yet."

"Don't worry. Blaze will do the honours, won't you?"

"Like I have a choice," he mumbled.

"Sorry, what did you say?" Daze glared at him.

"I said it would be my pleasure. What would you like, Jill?"

"A caramel latte, and a blueberry muffin, please."

"Mini or giant?"

"Need you ask?" Daze laughed.

While Blaze was waiting to be served, Daze and I found a vacant table.

"I hear the twins are starting a takeaway service?" she said.

"Yeah. From tomorrow, apparently. I have bad vibes about it."

"There you go." Blaze handed out the drinks and cakes.

"I'm going to be living in Washbridge," Daze said, before taking a bite of her mini strawberry muffin.

"How come?"

"The head of department wants all senior rogue retrievers to be based in the human world. They've been pressing us to make the move for some time, but I've resisted until now. Yesterday, I was given an ultimatum. If I don't make the move within a month, I'll be demoted."

"I take it you're not keen."

"I hate the idea."

"I'd love to live in the human world." Blaze chipped in. "I just can't afford it on my wages."

"I've arranged to meet another of the senior rogue retrievers here," Daze said. "She's been living in the human world for some time now. I thought she might be able to give me some tips."

"She's here now." Blaze pointed to a young woman

who'd just walked through the door. She had the same Amazonian build as Daze.

"Faze! Over here!" Daze called to her. "Blaze, go and get Faze a drink and a cake."

"I'll leave you to it." I stood up.

"Don't go, Jill," Daze said.

"Hi." Faze joined us.

"Faze, this is Jill Gooder."

"Pleased to meet you, Jill. Daze has told me a lot of good things about you."

"Daze tells me that you live in Washbridge."

"Yeah. I have an apartment in what used to be the old sock factory."

"How do you find living in the human world?" Daze asked.

"I'm not going to lie. It isn't easy. When I lived here in Candlefield, I could relax when I was off-duty. It's not so simple in Washbridge. The sups always treat me with suspicion, even when I'm not working. Take my apartment block. Everyone in there is a sup except for one female human. They often hold parties, but guess who's the only one who doesn't get invited? Me. They even invite the human. Even when I say good morning to someone, they look terrified."

"What do you do for a social life?" Daze asked.

"The only socialising I ever do is with other rogue retrievers. At least when you move to Washbridge, I'll have someone else to have a night out with."

"I really had better get going." I stood up. "Nice to meet you, Faze. Good luck with your move, Daze. See you, Blaze."

***

I'd managed to secure a meeting with the dean of Pixie Central College where Robbie Riddle had been a student until his unexplained disappearance. The college was tiny, so we'd arranged to meet on the playing fields at the rear of the building.

"Thank you for agreeing to see me, Dean."

"My pleasure. Robbie is one of our top students. We're all very concerned for his safety. And for the safety of the others who have gone missing."

"Others?"

"I assumed you would know. Two other students have disappeared in the last three months."

"I had no idea. Surely, the police must be investigating what has happened to them?"

"Unfortunately not. The police are adamant that the disappearances are not connected. It really isn't good enough."

"It's more than that. It's outrageous. Would you be prepared to give me details of the other two students? It might help me to piece together what has happened."

"Normally, I shouldn't, but given the circumstances, I'm prepared to do whatever it takes to help bring these students back safely. In fact, I anticipated that you'd ask that, so I brought these with me."

He handed me three folders which were so small that I would need a magnifying glass to study them.

"Thanks, Dean."

"No problem at all. If you need anything else, don't hesitate to contact me."

***

Back in Washbridge, everyone on the streets had their hands over their ears to drown out the noise. In Ever, the hysteria over Chameleon Wool appeared to have died down. Kathy was daydreaming behind the counter.

"What's that awful noise out there?" she asked.

"It's the Washbridge Bagpipe Festival; one of my neighbours is taking part. It looks like things have quietened down in here, though."

"Thank goodness. I couldn't handle that pandemonium every day."

"Where's the boss?"

"On the sun terrace—topping up her tan."

"Grandma!"

"Do you have to creep up on people like that?" I'd found her dozing on the sunbed.

"Sorry, I didn't realise that you were asleep." Snigger.

"I wasn't *asleep*. I was planning my next marketing campaign."

"Do you always snore when you're—?"

"Did you want something?"

"Yes. Have I told you about Jack's parents?"

"What about them?"

"They're teetotal. They don't approve of alcohol at all."

"That's fascinating, but why would I care?"

"I just thought it was interesting."

"I worry about you sometimes, young lady. Now, if you don't mind, I have more marketing to plan."

"That's not why I wanted to see you."

"Hurry up, then. I don't have all day."

"It's Jack's parents' golden wedding anniversary next weekend. You're invited to the party."

"A teetotal party? What's the point of that?"

"There'll be tea, coffee and soft drinks."

"Whoopee! How exciting. I think I'll pass."

"Oh? Well, if you're sure?"

"Is that it? Can I get back to work?"

"Yes, that's it. Thanks, Grandma."

Yay! Result!

***

My phone rang. It was Aunt Lucy.

"Jill. I have bad news about the anniversary party, I'm afraid."

"Don't tell me that you can't go?"

"I'll be there. Lester won't be able to make it, though. It seems that the annual grim reaper convention is on the same day. He doesn't feel that he can miss it. Needless to say, I'm not very impressed."

"Don't give him a hard time. He probably feels like he has to be there as he's new to the job."

"I suppose so. Anyway, I'm definitely coming. Have you spoken to the twins and Grandma yet?"

"The twins are coming, but no Alan or William."

"No surprises there. I'm not sure why those two bothered to get married."

"But the good news is that Grandma won't be coming."

"The teetotal thing worked, then?"

"Like a dream."

"Great. I'm looking forward to it even more now that I know that."

***

I was concerned about Megan, so I decided to pay a visit to the Washbridge offices of Love Bites.

"Hi?" The young female vampire behind reception looked surprised to see me.

"Hi. I wonder if I could talk to someone about your services?"

"I think you may have come to the wrong place. Love Bites is for vampires. You need Love Spell. I can give you their address, if you like?"

"No, thanks. I'm in the right place. I have two friends who have used your services to arrange dates. I'm just a little worried about them, and I was hoping to get some advice."

"I see. You need to speak to Scarlet. She's one of the owners."

"Is she in?"

"Yes. I'll just go and check if she has time to see you."

"Thanks."

A couple of minutes later, the receptionist reappeared. "Scarlet can spare you a few minutes. Through that door on the left."

Scarlet was an appropriate name for the woman who greeted me. Her bright red lipstick complimented her red hair. Her scarlet dress matched her high-heeled shoes.

"Scarlet Rose." She offered her hand. On her middle finger was a large ruby ring. "How can I help you?"

"I'm Jill Gooder. Two of my human friends have found matches through your agency."

"Recently?"

"Yes. Both of them."

"Luther, my accountant, met a lovely young woman named Maria. They seemed to get on well together, but Maria called it off because she found the temptation of human blood too much."

"That happens a lot, as you can imagine. Particularly for those who have never spent time in the human world before."

"Is there anything that can be done?"

Scarlet pulled open the drawer in her desk, and brought out a small cardboard box.

"Get Maria to try these patches."

"How do they work?"

"Very much like nicotine patches for those trying to give up smoking. These give a small infusion of synthetic blood. They don't work for everyone, but some vampires find it's enough to stave off the desire to attack a human."

"Thanks. How much do I owe you?"

"They're on the house. If they work, Maria can pop back here any time to buy further supplies. You said you had *two* friends who you wanted to discuss?"

"I think you may have solved both problems in one go. Could I get another box of these patches? And this time, you must let me pay."

Chapter 11

I'd arranged to meet with Gordon Rice, one of Douglas' younger brothers. Gordon and Jordan were identical twins. I knew from what Amy Rice had told me that Gordon was divorced and now lived alone. If his home was anything to go by, the family business must have been doing well. He lived in an apartment in Wash Tower; they certainly didn't come cheap.

"Come in." He greeted me at the door, wearing a black T-shirt and blue jeans.

"Nice place. Have you lived here long?"

"A couple of years—since Karen and I split up. Can I get you anything to drink?"

"No, thanks, I'm good."

He led the way to the living room.

"Thank you for seeing me today."

"No problem. I'm as eager as Amy to find out what happened to Doug."

"Of course. The initial reports seem to suggest it may have been an accident."

"I guess it's possible. If he really did slip and bang his head."

"You sound doubtful."

"I just don't understand what he was doing in there. Between the three of us, we work Monday to Saturday, but Sunday is our day off. On that particular day, though, Doug and I had arranged to go in to do some tidying up and routine maintenance. It's something we do every six months or so."

"Always you and Douglas?"

"Not necessarily. Our golden rule is that there are always

two of us on duty. Doug, Jordan and I work a rota during the normal working week."

"Jordan is your twin brother?"

"That's right. As I said, there are always two of us in on each working day. When it comes to the maintenance, it's whoever is free. This time around, it was supposed to be me and Doug."

"But you weren't there when it happened?"

"No. I got a call from Doug at the crack of dawn on the Sunday we were meant to be going in. It actually woke me up. He said he couldn't make it, so I just turned over and went back to sleep. I figured we'd rearrange it for another weekend. It's not as though it was urgent."

"Did he say why he couldn't make it?"

"No. I don't think so, but I was still half asleep."

"Didn't you consider going in by yourself?"

"No. Like I said, we have a golden rule that there must always be two of us there."

"In case one of you gets locked in the freezer?"

"That can't happen. The door can be unlocked from the inside, and even if that somehow failed, there's an alarm that can be triggered from in there."

"Which would fit with the theory that it was an accident, I guess. If your brother fell and knocked himself unconscious, he would have been unable to unlock the door or set off the alarm."

"But that still doesn't explain why he told me that he wasn't going in."

"Maybe he changed his mind later?"

"In that case, why didn't he call me back? He would have called me."

That same question was still buzzing around my head

after I'd left Wash Tower. From what Gordon had said, it was obvious that the three brothers were very safety conscious. The 'two-man' system should have ensured that accidents like this could not happen, or at least should not have proven fatal. Why had Douglas Rice decided to go into work after telling his brother he couldn't make it? Why risk working in the freezer alone?

I was beginning to smell a rat.

***

Back at my office, I was using my dad's old magnifying glass to study the three files which the dean of Pixie Central College had given to me. Robbie and the two other 'missing' pixies were not studying the same subjects, so did not take the same classes. I was beginning to think there was no connection between them, but then I read the supplementary pages at the back of the files, which listed their extracurricular activities. All three of them were members of the Human World Society. That seemed to gel with what both Maddy and Lionel had told me about Robbie being fascinated with the human world. I would need to pay another visit to the college, to speak to the other members of that society.

There was someone else I needed to catch up with first, though.

"Colonel? Colonel? Are you there?"

There was no sign of him, but then my office door flew open.

"Are you okay, Jill?" Jules looked concerned. "I thought I heard you shouting."

"I—err—I was just shouting at the cat. He was scratching my desk again."

"Oh?" Jules glanced across at Winky who was curled up, fast asleep on the sofa. "Okay, then. As long as you're alright."

"I'm fine, thanks."

I really would have to be more careful.

Just then, the temperature dropped, and the colonel's ghost appeared.

"Did you call, Jill?"

"I did."

"Sorry it took me a little while. I was ironing my trousers. I daren't trust Cilla with them; she scorched the last pair."

"I've spoken to my friend about the theft of your valuables, and she might be able to help, but she'll need a full description of all the items that have been taken. Photos too if you have them."

"No problem. Give me a day or so, and I'll let you have all the details. The sooner we get rid of this scoundrel, the happier Cilla and I will be. Thanks, again, Jill."

"What's your game?" Winky had jumped off the sofa and was giving me the evil eye.

"What do you mean?"

"I heard you tell the pretty, young thing that—"

"Her name is Jules."

"Whatever. I can't be expected to remember everyone's name. You told her that I'd been scratching your desk."

"Sorry. It was all I could think of on the spur of the moment."

"You can make up for it by giving us both some salmon."

"Both?"

"Me and Lenny." He pointed to the space next to him. "Who do you think?"

"Oh, right, sorry. I hadn't realised your friend was here again."

"Well he is, and we're both starving. So, if you wouldn't mind?"

"Okay." I put out the two bowls of salmon, and then made a call to Pixie Central College.

"The Dean's Office. Freda Fullglass speaking. How may I be of assistance?"

"Hi, my name is Jill Gooder. I came to see the dean earlier today. I wonder if I could have a quick word with him?"

"I'm sorry, Ms Gooder, but the dean has actually gone out. He won't be back until the day after tomorrow. I'm his PA. If you tell me what it's in connection with, I may be able to help."

"I've been looking through the files that he gave me, and I was hoping to find more information about the Human World Society."

"I won't be of much help with that, I'm afraid. There are so many out-of-hours clubs that it's hard to keep tabs on them all. What I can tell you though, is that they meet once a week, on Tuesdays at six pm."

"That's fine. I'll drop by then."

"Oh, and one more thing. The student who runs the club is called Barnaby Bandtime."

"Okay. Thanks very much."

I'd no sooner finished on the call than Mad walked through the door.

"Have you got a minute, Jill?"

"Sure. Come in."

"How come you have two desks out there, but no receptionists?"

"The two-desk thing is a long story. Jules is supposed to be out there. Maybe she just nipped to the loo. What can I do for you?"

"I need a favour. Actually, it's not for me. It's for Mum. She asked if I'd come and see you."

"How can I help?"

"I feel embarrassed to ask, but Mum will kill me if I don't."

"Go on."

"She's missing Nails really badly. Don't ask me why. Anyway, I just happened to mention that you knew the guy who owns the bottle top shop on the high street. You do, don't you?"

"Sort of. Norman and I have some history."

"Mum wondered if you'd have a word with him to see if he knows of any cure for those with a bottle top addiction. I realise it's a bit of a long shot."

"It's hardly in Norman's interest to cure the addicts, is it? They're boosting his profits."

"That's what I told her."

"I'll have a chat with him, but I don't hold out much hope."

"Thanks, Jill. You're a diamond. Do you want to organise another training session to see if we can get you over to Ghost Town?"

"Not just yet. I still haven't fully recovered from the last one."

"Okay. Let me know when you're ready." She stood up.

"By the way, Mad. I've spoken to the colonel. He's going to let me have a list of the stolen items in the next day or so."

"Great. I'll get straight on it once I've got that." She started for the door, but then hesitated. "Why has your cat got two bowls of food? Don't you think that's overdoing it a bit?"

"They're not both for him. One is for Lenny, the ghost cat."

"What ghost cat?"

"Isn't there a ghost cat standing next to Winky?"

"No. Just your one-eyed little beauty."

"Right. My mistake."

"Bye, Jill."

Winky was shuffling nervously towards the sofa.

"Where do you think you're going?"

"It's time for my nap."

"You lied to me! You told me Lenny was here."

"You must have misunderstood."

"Come to think of it, I've only actually seen your ghostly friend once. How many other times have you got me to give you double the food, under false pretences?"

"I'm so tired." He stretched and pretended to yawn. "I need to sleep."

And with that, the lying little so-and-so disappeared under the sofa.

***

On my way back home, I made a detour via Wash Point. I wanted to see the area of river from where Brendan Bowlings had gone missing. I had a distant memory of coming to the river with my mum and dad when I was a child — for a picnic, I think. I picked up the river a couple of miles outside of Washbridge city centre, and followed it downstream. Wash Point was about a mile and a half from the main road. En route, I came across numerous fishermen. Without exception, they were all very friendly. Several of them knew Brendan Bowlings — although none of them had seen him on the day that he went missing. My discussion with an old guy named Albert Mannings was typical.

"Brendan? Course I know him." He took a puff on his pipe. "Good fisherman is Brendan. Not as good as me, of course." He laughed.

I was standing downwind of Albert, and struggling to see him through the cloud of smoke belching from his pipe.

"You didn't see him on the day he went missing, though?"

"No. I was at the bowls that day."

"Ten pin?"

"Nah. That's not *real* bowling. I play crown green bowls for Washbridge Mavericks. It was the semi-final that day. We lost, but we were cheated."

"I don't suppose you have any idea what might have become of Brendan?"

"I reckon he must have found himself a bit on the side, and done a runner."

"What makes you say that?"

"That's what usually happens, isn't it? That's why my Blanche threw me out."

"You were seeing someone else?"

"Yeah. Blanche found out, and gave me my marching orders."

"So, you're with your other — err — lady friend, now?"

"Nah. She went off with someone else. I'm all on my own now." He grinned. "Do you fancy coming for a drink with me?"

"Thanks, but I'm with someone." I began to edge away. "Thanks for your help."

A few minutes later, I reached the fence, which had effectively cut off a stretch of the river.

"It should never have been allowed!" A fisherman, who had set up only a few metres away, shouted. "One of the best stretches of fishing is inside there." He pointed to the eight-foot high fence which was topped with razor wire. "Someone on the council got a backhander; that's what I think."

"Do you know who the factory belongs to?"

"No idea. There's no name on the building anywhere. It's a liberty, if you ask me. And this thing is no compensation." He pointed to the footbridge. "They built two of them."

I crossed the river using the newly built footbridge. Once on the other side, I followed the fence for a twenty metres or so. At that point, it took a ninety degree turn, back towards the main building. Beyond that point access to the river was restored, so I crossed over again using the second footbridge. Through the fence, I could see the factory building, which was of a red brick construction. There was no name on the building, and as far as I could see, not a single window.

Very strange. Very strange indeed.

Chapter 12

The next morning, Jack was eating muesli for breakfast.

"How can you eat that stuff?" I pulled a face.

"It's good for you."

"Says who?"

"All the experts."

"I bet they don't eat it—these so-called experts. I bet *they* have a fry-up for breakfast."

"Have you even tried it?"

"I don't need to. I have eyes in my head."

"Mmm, lovely!" He put a spoonful of the horrible stuff into his mouth. "By the way, you haven't forgotten I'm away overnight on a course the day after tomorrow, have you?"

"You're always going away on courses. I'm beginning to think you have another woman hidden away somewhere."

"I don't go away that often, and besides, where would I find someone as beautiful as you." He leaned forward and tried to kiss me.

"Yuk! Get away from me with your muesli-covered lips."

"Do you have the final numbers for the anniversary party?" he said through a mouthful of wood shavings.

"I had them ready for you last night, as promised, but you weren't here."

"I had to work late. There was an incident in West Chipping town centre."

"An *incident*? Very cloak and dagger."

"I can't say any more. It's on a need-to-know basis."

"That's okay. I don't want to know, on an *I-don't-care* basis."

"So? Is everyone coming?"

"Not quite. It's just Kathy and Peter, Aunt Lucy, and the twins."

"What about the other menfolk?"

"Alan and William both have to work. And Lester has to attend a grim—err—a convention."

"Why would he want to go to a convention if it's going to be so grim?"

"Err—it's not Lester who thinks it'll be grim. He's quite excited about it. It was Aunt Lucy who said it would be grim."

"What is it Lester does, exactly?"

"Lester?"

"Yeah. What does he do?"

"What does *Lester* do?"

"Is it top secret or something?"

"No, of course not. Lester—err—he—err despatches things. That's it. He works in a despatch department."

"Oh? And this convention is to do with his work?"

"Yes. It's a despatcher's convention. It sounds deadly dull to me."

"No kidding. I can see why your aunt thinks it's grim. What about your grandmother?"

"Grandma? What about her?"

"Will she be coming to the party?"

"She wanted to, but she'll be out of town on that day. She's going to a convention, too."

"The same one as Lester?"

"No. This is something to do with yarn. She was devastated that she can't make it, and sends her apologies."

"Not to worry. I'll let Mum know who'll be there."

What? I know I was lying. I don't need a guilt trip from you. And besides, I was doing it to protect Jack. From

Grandma.

Jack left before I did. He no doubt had work to do on his top secret *incident*.

"I'm glad I caught you, Jill," Mr Hosey said.

That made one of us. His stupid train, Bessie, was blocking my driveway. Again.

"I'm just on my way to work, Mr Hosey."

"This won't take a minute. I tried to catch Jack, but he said he was working on something important, but that you weren't particularly busy, and would have time to talk to me."

Jack. Was. So. Dead.

"He must have been joking. I'm really busy just now."

"You may be busy today, but who's to say what next week will bring? Or next month? The only way to ensure your business has a constant flow of customers is to−?" He looked to me for the answer.

"Advertise?"

"Got it in one, Jill. And that's precisely why I wanted to talk to you."

Only then, did I notice that Mr Ivers' movie newsletter ads were no longer displayed on the train.

"Fortuitously for you, I find myself with an opening in my advertising schedule. I know how disappointed you were to miss out on an opportunity to advertise on Bessie last time."

"How come Mr Ivers has taken his ads down?"

"It seems he's abandoned his movie newsletter. He did beg me to allow him to advertise his new venture, but I had to turn him down."

"The bottle top newsletter?"

"You've heard about it, then. I didn't want to be a party to encouraging that wicked addiction."

Huh?

"So, you see, that's why I'm able to offer you this opportunity of a lifetime."

"Sorry, Mr Hosey, but it isn't for me."

"Have you forgotten that it includes free rides on Bessie?"

"Tempting as that is, I have to decline."

"Just don't blame me if your business goes under." He walked off in a huff.

***

I'd arranged to meet Maria at Cuppy C, but there was no sign of her when I arrived. The twins were nowhere to be seen, either.

"Where are they?" I asked the assistant who was manning the tea room counter.

"Amber and Pearl? They're both out on deliveries."

"Oh, yeah. I'd forgotten the delivery service had started. How's it—?"

The phone behind the counter rang, so the assistant broke off from serving me.

"Cuppy C U Soon. Gillian speaking. How can I help?" She grabbed a pen, and began scribbling notes onto a pad. "What flavour? Mini or giant? Can you give me your address, please? Okay. We'll be with you as soon as possible."

"It's been like that all day," she said when she came back to the counter. "I've barely seen Amber or Pearl. I don't know how I'm supposed to take a break."

"Did I hear right? Was that an order for a single muffin?"

"Yeah. A mini one."

"Have you had many small orders?"

"The majority have been like that. One cupcake here, one muffin there, one cup of tea."

Oh dear.

The phone rang another three times while I was waiting for Maria to arrive.

"Sorry I'm late, Jill." She sounded out of breath. "The pig got out."

"You have a pig?"

"I don't. It's my brother's. It's one of those miniature ones. It had got into next door's garden. They weren't very impressed because it had done its business in their dahlias."

"Oh dear. Can I get you a drink?"

"Not for me. I can't stay long."

"This shouldn't take more than a couple of minutes. I just wanted to follow up on our conversation of the other day. About you and Luther."

"I know you mean well, Jill. And Luther is a lovely man, but I don't see how it's ever going to work."

"There may be a way." I took the cardboard box from my pocket.

"What are those?"

"I got them from Love Bites. You're not the only vampire to run into this kind of problem."

"Patches?"

"Yeah. They slow release synthetic blood. According to the woman at Love Bites, these should get rid of your craving, and over time, you'll find you can do without them."

"I'm not sure about this." She studied the box.

"You like Luther, don't you?"

"Yes. He's really nice."

"Well then. Give them a go. What do you have to lose?"

Maria still seemed sceptical, but she agreed to give them a shot.

***

Back in Washbridge, I made my way down the high street to Norman's new shop, Top Of The World. It was still early, but the shop was already doing a brisk trade. Norman had taken on a couple of assistants. The man himself was standing in one corner, monitoring proceedings.

"Good morning, Norman."

He treated me to his usual 'out-to-lunch' expression for a few seconds before the penny dropped. "Oh, hi."

"Is there somewhere we can talk in private?"

"There's the toilet."

"Err—I was thinking more your office."

"Oh? Okay." He led the way.

"I need your help, Norman. I realise this may sound like a strange question, but have you ever come across any—err—bottle top addicts?"

"Oh yeah," he said, quite matter-of-factly. "It gets a few people like that."

"I suppose they must be your best customers?"

"No." He shook his head. "That sort of thing is bad for the industry. That's why Toppers Anonymous was formed—it's funded by the industry."

"Toppers Anonymous?"

"They help people with a bottle top addiction."

"Do they have a local branch?"

"Yeah. Would you like one of their cards?"

"That would be great."

Who would have thought it? Maybe there was hope for Deli and Nails' marriage after all.

I made a call to Mad to give her the good news.

She was delighted, and promised to pass the information on to Nails straight away.

As I made my way back up the high street, I noticed there was a queue of people outside Betty Longbottom's shop, which had now reverted to its original name: She Sells.

Betty must have seen me looking through the window because she came outside to join me.

"Don't let me drag you away, Betty. I can see you have a lot of customers."

"It's okay. I have two assistants working for me now. They can cope."

"Business seems to be booming. Have you been doing a lot of advertising?"

"None, but I have had a spot of good luck."

"Oh?"

"Have you heard of Viv Royal?"

"I don't think so. Should I have?"

"She's a megastar on YouTube. She has millions of subscribers. Anyway, she's decided that crustacean jewellery is the hot thing. Ever since she started to wear it, business has been booming."

"That's great. I'm really pleased for you."

"Did I see you just come out of Norman's shop?"

"Yeah."

"I didn't realise you'd become a topper. You have to be careful with those bottle tops, Jill. They can be addictive."

"I'll bear that in mind." I glanced up the road. "I see The Final Straw has closed down."

"It's a real shame. I loved their drinks. No one else does flavours like they did."

***

Mrs V and Jules were both in today. Neither of them looked very happy.

"Have you two been falling out again?"

"No." Jules spoke first.

"It's your grandmother's new product," Mrs V said.

"Chameleon Wool? What's wrong with it?"

"You might well ask." She held up an off-white scarf.

"That's rather plain for you, isn't it?"

"It wasn't plain until this morning. It *was* multi-coloured. The colours just disappeared."

"Yes." Jules chimed in. "Look." She held up a pair of anaemic-looking socks.

"What's happened?"

"That's what we'd like to know." Mrs V picked up the phone. "We've been trying to contact the Chameleon Wool hotline, but all we can get is your grandmother's voice telling us how important our call is to her. It's not good enough, Jill. All of our work will have been wasted if the colours are permanently lost. Can't you have a word?"

"I don't think that would help the situation. I'm sure Grandma is on it."

I hurried through to my office. I had more than enough on my plate without getting involved with Grandma's business problems.

"Didn't I tell you!" Winky was doing a little jig, and holding something in his paw.

"Why are you so happy?"

"Didn't I tell you that I was going to win the lottery?"

"Pull the other one."

"It's true." He stopped dancing, and held up the lottery ticket. "Granted I didn't win the jackpot, but I have won five thousand pounds for getting five numbers."

"Really? Are you sure?"

"Of course I am. Five thousand smackeroos, and they're all mine."

"Well, congratulations, I guess. I'm glad one of us has some luck."

"I'll need you to cash it in for me."

"Why me? Cash it in yourself."

"How can I? I'm a cat."

"You managed to buy it."

"I got a friend's two-legged to get it for me. Come on, Jill. I need the cash."

"What's my cut?"

"Why should you get any?"

"For the wear and tear on my shoes."

"The shop is only two doors down."

"Ten per cent."

"How can you do that to your darling cat?"

"You mean the *darling cat* who has been conning me all week? I haven't forgotten the Lenny incident."

"Okay. Ten per cent."

Result! Five hundred pounds just for cashing in a lottery

ticket. Who's the smart one now?

Don't answer that.

I took the ticket, and slipped it into my handbag. "I'm not sure when I'll be able to get your cash, though, because I'm run off my feet."

"No problem. I'm a patient guy."

Chapter 13

With Sheila Bowlings' permission, I'd already looked through her husband's personal papers that he kept at the house. Now she'd cleared it with his employer for me to visit his place of work, to check any personal papers he might have there. Brendan Bowlings worked for Washbridge Council in the Weights and Measures office (whatever that was).

"It's just terrible." His secretary, a fussy little woman, greeted me.

"I'm sorry. I didn't catch your name?"

"Sarah Weller. I've been Brendan's secretary for almost ten years. I can't believe this has happened." She was close to tears. "Do you think he is — ?"

She didn't finish the question, but then she didn't need to because it was quite obvious what she was thinking.

"It's too early to speculate on what might have happened to him."

"I'm very worried. Brendan wouldn't have simply left without a word."

"There was nothing bothering him, then? As far as you know?"

"No. He was perfectly happy."

"I believe that his wife called earlier, and cleared it for me to look through his personal things."

"Yes, of course. Please come with me." She led the way to another small room. "This is Brendan's office."

"Thank you. Do you think I could get a drink?" I wanted her out of the room, and that was the politest way I could think of to get her out from under my feet.

"Of course. Tea? Coffee?"

"Tea with one and two-thirds spoonfuls of sugar, please."

"One and — err — ? Okay. I'll be right back."

It didn't take very long to look through all the drawers in his desk. All but one of them contained nothing but council documents. The bottom drawer on the right-hand side appeared to be the one where he kept all his personal papers. There were credit card statements and numerous receipts. Rather than trying to scrutinise them under the beady eye of his secretary, I slipped them into my bag.

"There you are." She held out the cup. "I think I've got the sugar right."

"Thanks, but I've just had an urgent call. I have to leave straight away."

"But what about your tea?"

"Sorry." I made for the door. "I really do have to run."

***

"Can't you have a word with your grandmother?" Mrs V collared me as soon as I got back to the office. "It's impossible to get through on the support line."

"The Chameleon Wool is still not working, I take it?"

"It keeps coming and going." She picked up the same scarf she'd shown me earlier. "Look!"

Different sections of the scarf kept changing colour. One moment a section would be red, blue or green, and then the next it would be back to the anaemic-looking shade of off-white.

"I'll pop down there in a while, but I have some papers to look through first. Don't expect too much, though. Grandma rarely takes any notice of me."

"Where is it?" Winky demanded, as soon as I stepped into my office.

"Where is what?" I snapped back.

"The lottery cash, of course."

"I haven't had a chance to claim it yet. I told you it might take me a while. In case you haven't noticed, I'm really busy."

"You need to prioritise."

"And I suppose your lottery cash would be top priority."

"It goes without saying, doesn't it?"

"I'll get around to it as soon as I can. It's not as though anyone is going to run away with it, is it?"

"I hope you have the ticket in a safe place?"

"Yes! It's in my bag. Now, if you don't mind, I have work to do."

I emptied all the papers that I'd found in Brendan Bowlings' drawer, onto my desk, and began to work my way through them. They made for very interesting reading. There were a number of credit card statements among them, and interestingly, although the card was a personal one, not a business one, they were addressed to his office. I'd seen other credit card statements at his home, but a quick look through these suggested that this card had been used mainly for restaurants, theatres and clothes shops — women's clothes shops. There were also a lot of receipts. One in particular caught my eye; it was for a double room in a hotel in Brighton, dated two weeks earlier. A quick check against the credit card statement confirmed that payment had been made with that card. It was time to make a call to Sheila Bowlings. This could potentially be a little awkward; all my powers of diplomacy would be required.

What? Of course I can be diplomatic. Sheesh!

"Sheila? It's Jill Gooder."

"Have you found him? Is he okay?"

"No, sorry. No news yet, I'm afraid. I was just wondering if you or Brendan had been away recently."

"Yes, a couple of weeks ago. To my sister's."

"Where does she live?"

"In Cambridge. Brendan didn't go with me. He and Maude don't get on."

"What did your husband do while you were at your sister's?"

"He stayed at home and watched the racing, like he always does. Why do you ask?"

"No reason. Thanks for that. I'll be in touch when I know anything."

I quickly ended the call before she could ask any awkward questions. If the dates matched up, and my guess was that they would, it looked like Brendan had been living a secret life that his wife knew nothing about. If he hadn't been with his wife in Brighton, who had he been with?

Jules popped her head around the door. "Jill, I have Mr Whiteside to see you."

"Okay. Give me a minute, and then send him in."

Zac Whiteside was my landlord. I couldn't let him see Winky, or I'd be looking for a new office. Luckily for me, Winky had curled up under the sofa, and was now fast asleep. Provided he didn't stir, Zac would never notice him.

"Thanks for seeing me without an appointment," Zac said.

"No problem. I'm not behind on the rent, am I?"

"No, nothing like that. It's just that I've spent a lot of time recently reflecting on my life, and where exactly I'm headed."

"Oh?" Why was he telling me that? Did he have me mixed up with a shrink?

"Anyway, I've decided to sell up and move on. I'm going to join a commune in the South of France."

"Wow! That's quite the lifestyle change."

"I'm letting all my tenants know that I've sold all the properties in my portfolio to Macabre Holdings."

"I'm not mad on the name."

"It's not as sinister as it might sound. The company is named after the owner, Martin Macabre. He'll no doubt come around soon to introduce himself."

"Right. Well, thanks for letting me know, Zac. And good luck with your new life."

"That's a made-up name, if ever I heard one." Winky came out from under the sofa. "Martin Macabre? Do me a favour."

"You'll need to stay on your toes. We can't afford to let the new landlord see you when he comes around."

"No problem. I'll be as nimble as a ninja."

***

I couldn't put it off any longer. Mrs V had been chuntering away ever since I came back to the office.

"I'm going down to Ever, to see Grandma."

"Good!" Mrs V held up the scarf, which was once again totally devoid of colour. "This really isn't good enough, Jill."

There was still a queue outside She Sells. The YouTube starlet had certainly done Betty a big favour.

There was a queue at Ever too, but these were not customers waiting to buy stuff. They were all up in arms about the recent problems with Chameleon Wool. I felt really sorry for Kathy and Chloe who were desperately trying to pacify the crowd. Grandma, of course, was nowhere to be seen. Normally, I might have tried the roof terrace, but I doubted she'd be up there today. It would have been far too easy for the angry customers to track her down up there.

Just as I suspected, she was in her office.

"Shut the door, quick!" she shouted, as soon as I walked in.

"It's not fair for you to hide in here while Kathy and Chloe have to take all the flak."

"I'm not hiding! I'm trying to sort out the problem."

"It doesn't look as though you're having much joy."

"Is that why you came down here? To state the obvious, and to gloat?"

"I'm not gloating. I promised Mrs V and Jules that I'd talk to you. They've been trying to get through on the support line for hours."

"Them and everyone else." She picked up a sheet of paper which appeared to contain the details of a very complex spell.

"Is that the Chameleon Wool spell?"

"No, it's my shopping list. Of course it is!"

"Can I see it?"

"What good would that do?"

"None probably, but how can it hurt?"

"Here then!" She shoved the sheet of paper into my hand.

I was used to concocting quite complex spells of my own, but this was something else entirely. It took me several minutes just to figure out how it worked. It was incredibly clever.

"Aren't those two the wrong way around?" I pointed to two of the dozens of images that went to make up the spell.

"Don't be ridiculous."

"The butterfly and the marigold." I pointed again. "Shouldn't they be — ?"

"What are you talking about?" Grandma snatched it back, and studied the spell again. After a few minutes, she nodded her head. "You could be right." She closed her eyes, and I could see she was casting the spell.

Moments later, a huge cheer went up from inside the shop. I cracked the door open just wide enough to see the crowd gathered around the counter.

"It's working!" someone yelled.

"About time, too."

Slowly, the customers began to file out of the shop, leaving Kathy and Chloe with a relieved look on their faces.

I turned to Grandma. "It worked."

"Such a big fuss about nothing."

"You're welcome."

"I would have sorted it out myself if you hadn't come barging in, disturbing my concentration."

The woman was unbelievable.

***

When I arrived home, Megan was just coming out of her house. She was wearing a polo neck jumper, and it seemed like she was trying to avoid my gaze.

"Hi, Megan."

"Oh? Hey, Jill. I didn't see you there."

I knew very well that she had.

"Are you okay?"

"Yes, thanks. I'm meeting someone in town."

"Your new boyfriend?"

"Err—yeah."

"What's his name?"

"Ryan."

"Is he the one you met through the dating agency? How's it going with him?"

"He is, and it's going okay, thanks."

Somehow, that didn't ring true.

"Where does he work?"

"He's the manager of the betting shop on the high street."

"WashBets?"

She nodded. "I'm sorry, Jill, I have to get going or I'll be late."

That was not the Megan Lovemore I'd come to know. Until recently, she'd always been bright and bubbly, and if anything, too chatty. But that had all changed since she'd started dating Ryan, and having seen the bruise on her neck, I thought I knew why. It was high time I introduced myself to that young man.

I was just about to go into the house when a car pulled up onto what had been Mrs Rollo's drive. A young man, no more than twenty-years of age, jumped out.

"Hi!" he shouted. His hair was spiked up with way too much gel. He was wearing jeans, and a T-shirt with the words: 'Life Is Short' on the front.

"I'm Jill Gooder." I walked over to greet him.

"Pleased to meet you, Jill. I'm Dominic Worms; everyone calls me Worms."

"Really? Okay, well it's nice to meet you, Worms. I take it you're renting this place?"

"Yeah. I'll be moving in on Sunday, hopefully."

"Are you from around here?"

"No, can't you tell by the accent? I come from down south, but I'm a student at Washbridge College. This is my final year, and my parents thought I'd be able to revise better here—away from all the noise of the dorms. They're footing the bill."

"It's rather big just for you, isn't it?"

"It'll be nice to have some space. Those dorms are like prison cells."

"Well, I hope you enjoy your stay."

Chapter 14

"What's going on out there?" Jack tried to cover his ears with the pillow.

It was stupid o' clock on Monday morning, and the music was so loud that it felt as though the house was vibrating.

I got out of bed and walked over to the window. "It's next door."

"Megan?"

"No. The other side. I meant to mention that our new neighbour was moving in yesterday."

"Who is it?"

"Worms."

"Who?"

"His name is Dominic Worms. He introduced himself when I got home from work the other day. He's a student in his last year at Washbridge College. He seemed quite nice."

"I'm not impressed." Jack came and joined me at the window. "How many of them are there out there?"

"A lot by the looks of it."

There were cars parked all down the road, blocking most of the driveways. Young men and women, most of them with a drink in their hand, had spilled out onto next door's front garden. Meanwhile, the music—and I use the term loosely—was getting even louder.

I took a look out of the back window.

"It's the same out here. The back garden is full of them. Come back, Mrs Rollo. All is forgiven. Even your baking."

"I'll go around there, and have a word." Jack reached for his jeans.

"No. Leave it. It's his first night. He's probably just

celebrating. I'm sure it will settle down after tonight."

"Okay. I'll go and make us a cup of tea."

The party finally ended around four o' clock, which explains why neither Jack nor I woke until almost nine.

"Look at the time!" Jack shouted as he threw on some clothes. "I'm meant to be in a meeting at nine-thirty."

"Aren't you going to have a shower?"

"No. They'll just have to put up with my B.O."

What a charmer.

One of the few advantages of working for myself was that I got to decide my own hours. It was almost a quarter to ten by the time I was ready to leave the house. It was only then I remembered that I needed to buy some custard creams to take into the office with me. I'd eaten the last few the previous afternoon.

Little Jack Corner was standing on his box behind the counter in the corner shop.

"Good morning, young lady. What can I get for you, today?"

"Just these." I grabbed two packets of custard creams.

"You timed your visit very well because I've just introduced a new service that is going to be in great demand."

"What's that?"

"I've started a VHS lending library."

"VHS? You mean videos?"

"Yes. Only the most modern technology. None of that Betamax rubbish." He pointed to the far side of the shop. "Have you seen the range of movies on offer?"

"Isn't it all downloads and streaming nowadays?"

"Downloads?"

"Netflix. That type of thing?"

"Do they offer VHS?"

"Probably not."

"Well then. They're well behind the curve. So, can I interest you in a subscription?"

"Thanks, but no. We don't do much viewing at home. Bye, then."

"Don't go until you've heard my thought for the day."

"Oh, yes. I'd almost forgotten."

"Too many cooks have a silver lining."

"Great. Thanks for that."

***

When I got back to the house, our young next-door neighbour was in his garden.

"Can I have a word?" I shouted.

"Sure." He came over. "I know what you're going to say, and I'd like to apologise for last night. Things got a little out of hand. I invited a handful of friends over to toast the new house, and well—we got a little carried away."

"The music was rather loud."

"I know, and I'm sorry. It won't happen again."

"No problem. You're only young once."

"Thanks for being so understanding."

It was good to have cleared the air. It seemed that my first impression of our new neighbour had been right after all. He wasn't a bad sort.

As I was running late, I didn't bother to call in at the office. Instead, I went straight to Jordan Rice's place.

Wow! What a contrast to his twin brother, Gordon,

whose top-end apartment was in one of the most sought after developments in Washbridge. Jordan Rice was living in a tiny bedsit, which was rather squalid. As he led the way inside, I noticed he walked with a slight limp.

"Motorcycle accident when I was a teenager." He must have caught me staring at his leg. "I apologise for the state of this place. The wife and I split up recently. This is just a stopgap until I get something more permanent."

"I'm sorry to hear that."

He shrugged. "These things happen. Do you want something to drink?"

I declined. If the crockery was as clean as the rest of the bedsit, I had no intention of drinking from it.

"I don't really understand why you're here." He lit a cigarette.

"Amy has asked me to investigate Douglas' death."

"There can't be much doubt about what happened, can there? He should never have been at work by himself. It's our golden rule."

"Gordon told me about that. Why do you think Douglas would have broken it?"

"I don't know. Doug was usually ultra-cautious about everything." Jordan fought back a tear.

"How is the business doing?"

"Okay. It's tough for everyone these days."

"Does the business have any cash problems?"

"No. What does that have to do with what happened to Doug?"

"Probably nothing. How had Douglas seemed to you, recently?"

"His usual self."

"He hadn't mentioned any problems?"

"No! Look, this was an accident. A tragic accident. I don't see the point of any of this."

That was pretty much his reaction to the rest of my questions. It was quite obvious that as far as Jordan Rice was concerned, his brother's death had been an accident. And so far, I'd found nothing to suggest otherwise.

***

Amber and Pearl were both behind the counter in the tea room at Cuppy C.

"No deliveries today?" I asked.

"Muffin?" Amber said.

"I thought you'd both be whizzing around Candlefield on your scooters."

"Caramel latte?" Pearl grabbed a cup.

Something wasn't right. They had both deliberately ignored my questions.

"Yeah. A blueberry muffin. Giant not mini. And a caramel latte, please."

I waited until I had my drink and cake.

"And now I'd like to know what's going on with the deliveries. The last time I was in here, your assistant told me you were booked solid all day. What's happened?"

"We had a board meeting last night," Amber said. "And we took an executive decision to cancel the delivery service."

"Already? It's only been running for a day."

"Things didn't quite pan out as we'd expected."

"You mean that people were ordering a single muffin or a single cup of tea?"

"Something like that."

"I did warn you."

"No one likes a know-it-all, Jill." Amber pouted.

"Anyway, that's all history now," Pearl said. "During our board meeting, we came up with another brilliant idea."

Would they never learn?

"What now?"

"You could at least pretend to be excited," Amber continued to pout.

"You have had rather a lot of brilliant ideas, and to be fair, not many of them have turned out so well."

"This one is different."

Weren't they all? "Go on, then."

"If you're just going to make fun, there's no point," Pearl said.

"I won't. I promise."

"Swear on this blueberry muffin." Amber held out the plate.

"Do what?"

"Go on. And, if you do make fun of our new idea, you'll be banned from ever having another muffin in Cuppy C."

That was a serious threat. My first reaction was to let them keep their secret, but curiosity got the better of me. I would just have to be ultra-careful how I reacted. No matter how hare-brained the scheme was, I couldn't afford to laugh. A muffin ban was a very serious sanction.

"We're going to host exhibitions by local artists in Cuppy C," Amber announced, proudly.

"Paintings and sculptures," Pearl said. "That kind of thing."

"Actually, girls, that's not a bad idea. In fact, it's a really good idea."

"Are you just saying that, so we don't ban you from eating muffins?" Pearl eyed me suspiciously.

"No, honestly, I think it's a great idea. Probably your best to-date."

The twins both beamed with pride.

"We already have our first exhibition lined up," Pearl said.

"Yeah. It's later this week." Amber sounded every bit as enthusiastic.

"That's great. I'll call in and take a look at it."

"Oh, while I remember, Jill." Pearl passed my coffee. "Mum said we should ask you to drop in to see her the next time you came into the shop."

"Any idea what it's about?"

"No, but she said it wasn't urgent."

***

When I arrived at Aunt Lucy's, I found her hard at work sewing. She had a pile of what appeared to be Lester's trousers beside her on the sofa.

"You look busy."

"It's that stupid job of Lester's. He spends a lot of time on his knees."

"Why?"

She gave me an *'isn't it obvious'* look.

"Sorry. Yes, I suppose he would."

"We can't afford to keep buying new pairs, so I'm sewing leather patches on these. He isn't very keen on the idea, but he'll just have to suck it up." Aunt Lucy looked up from what she was doing. "Or get a different job."

I doubted she'd ever come to terms with the idea that her

husband was working as a grim reaper.

"The twins said you wanted to see me."

"Actually, it's Barry who wants to see you."

"Oh? What about?"

"I think I should let him tell you. He's asleep upstairs. He had a long walk this morning."

"Barry!"

The sound of snoring was deafening.

"Barry!"

"What? Where?" He jumped up, but was obviously still half asleep. "Who did it?"

"It's me."

He was trying hard to focus. "Jill? I was having a lovely dream about a squirrel."

"Were you chasing it?"

"No. We were playing snakes and ladders."

"Right. Aunt Lucy said you wanted to see me."

"Yeah! This is so exciting." He spun around and around in circles.

"Slow down! What's so exciting?"

"The competition, of course. I'm going to win it. First prize."

"What competition is that?"

He walked over to the corner of the room, and then returned with a newspaper in his mouth. It was a week-old copy of The Candle.

"I want to enter, Jill. The first prize is a year's supply of Barkies."

No wonder he was so keen; he was crazy about Barkies. It was a competition to find the best photo of a pet dog.

"Can I enter, Jill? Can I? Please can I enter?"

"Sure, why not?" I took out my phone. "I'll take a photo now and send it in."

"No!" He raised a paw.

"What's wrong?"

"No offence, Jill, but are you a professional photographer?"

"Well, no, but—"

"I'm never going to win with just any old photo. I need a photograph taken by a professional."

"I wouldn't know where—"

"Here." He pushed a small business card towards me; it was for a company called Canine Shoots.

"This looks expensive."

"Please, Jill. You spend a lot of money on Hamlet. I really want this. Please!"

"Okay. I'll give them a call."

"Thank you, Jill." He launched himself at me. "I'm going to win those Barkies."

I was such a soft touch.

Once I was outside, I called the number on the card.

"Canine Shoots, Terry Eyre speaking."

Terrier? Seriously? "Hi, I'm enquiring about getting a photo of my dog. It's for the competition in The Candle."

"Oh, yes. I've done a lot of photos for that competition already."

"Good. I was wondering if you could tell me how much it would cost?"

He did, and it looked like I was going to need a second job to pay for it.

Chapter 15

Back at the office, Jules was all by herself.

"No Mrs V?"

"She and Armi have gone to Grimsby."

"Oh? Any particular reason?"

"Apparently, Armi is interested in fishing trawlers, and he's arranged for the two of them to go out on one today."

"On a fishing trawler? Aren't they rather smelly? I don't think I'd fancy that."

"Me neither. Annabel didn't seem very keen, but she didn't want to disappoint Armi."

"It's really windy today, too. I don't think I'd want to go to sea on a day like this."

"She said she'd bring us back some haddock."

"Nice. How's the Chameleon Wool going?"

"It's fine now." Jules held up a multi-coloured sock. "It looks like your grandmother must have sorted out the teething problems."

"Did you collect my lottery winnings?" Winky was on my case as soon as I walked into the office.

"I'm really sorry. I forgot."

"How could you forget my five thousand pounds?"

"I've been really busy, but I promise I'll get it in the morning."

"Swear on your muffins."

"Don't *you* start with that."

I made a phone call to Hotel Lexicon, the hotel in Brighton where Brendan Bowlings had spent the weekend while his wife was away at her sister's. The call proved to be a waste of time because they wouldn't answer any of my questions. If I wanted to get any information, I would have to pay them a visit.

"Your accountant is here." Jules' voice came through the intercom. "He says he isn't here on business."

"Send him in please, Jules."

Luther looked so much happier than the last time I'd seen him.

"I just wanted to come by and thank you, Jill. Whatever you said to Maria, it did the trick."

"You're back together?"

"Yes. She contacted me out of the blue, and said she'd like to give it another go. I couldn't be happier. How did you manage it?"

"It wasn't difficult. She already knew what a great guy you are."

"Now you're making me blush."

"It's true. It was just a case of cold feet."

"Well, whatever you said or did, I'm really grateful. Your next two monthly accounting sessions will be on the house."

"I can't let you do that."

"I insist."

"Okay, then. If you're sure?"

"I'm positive."

Result! That should pay for Barry's photographs.

"When are you seeing Maria again?"

"At the weekend. We went out last night, and had a great time. And, I discovered something about her I didn't know."

Oh dear.

"Apparently, she used to be a smoker. I had no idea until I spotted the patch on her arm. I'm glad she decided to give it up. Smoking really is bad for you."

"From what I hear, those patches work wonders."

***

Luther's mention of the patches had reminded me that there was someone else I needed to have a talk with.

WashBets was at the far end of the high street, in between the Sushi Bar and the dry cleaners. I'd never set foot inside a betting shop before—it was quite an experience. A dozen or more men, most of them middle-aged, were glued to the various TV screens on the wall. Some of them watched in silence, chewing their nails. Others screamed at the horses on screen—urging them on.

"Yeah?" The woman behind the counter looked as though her soul had been sucked out of her body.

"I'd like to speak to Ryan, please."

"The manager?"

"I guess so."

"If it's a complaint, you need to speak to his assistant, Bryan."

"It's not a complaint. It's a private matter."

"Oh?" For the first time, she showed a flicker of interest. "Are you his girlfriend?"

"No. Would you tell him it's about Megan."

"Wait there." She disappeared through one of the doors at the back of the building. Moments later, she reappeared followed by a tall man—a vampire.

"What's this about?" He came to the counter. "Is Megan alright?"

"She's fine. I just need a quiet word."

He gestured to a door on my side of the counter.

"What's going on?" he demanded, once we were inside the small office. "Who are you?"

Ryan was a good-looking guy with a great physique. Not the type I would have expected to use a dating agency. But then I could have said the same about Megan.

"Megan is my next-door neighbour."

"So?"

"I'm concerned about her. I've seen the bruising on her neck."

He flinched. "That was — err — I — err — didn't mean to — err — "

"Bite her? It's a bit late for that, isn't it?"

"She's the first human I've dated."

"A good looking guy like you? I find that hard to believe."

"It's true. I've dated a few vampires since I moved to the human world, but Megan is the first human. I met her through Love Bites. It's a — "

"I know what it is."

"I never thought that dating a human would be so difficult. The temptation is way greater than I thought it would be."

"So, you bit her and drank her blood?"

"It was only the once, and I only had a sip. When she screamed, it brought me to my senses and I stopped straight away."

"I'm surprised she didn't report you to the police, or at least dump you."

"I told her it was a love bite, and that I'd got carried away. I feel really guilty about it."

"You should have called the relationship off."

"I know, but I really do like Megan. She's a great girl. Are you going to call in the rogue retrievers?"

"I should." I was unsure what to do. He did seem genuinely sorry for what he'd done. "Here. Take these." I handed him the box. "Use these patches. They should help to control the urge, but if they don't, then you'll have to call it off."

"Okay. Thanks. I will."

"I'll be watching Megan, and if I see one more cut or bruise on her neck—"

"You won't. I promise."

***

Using magic to get around the human world wasn't something I normally liked to do, but I was so busy that I didn't have time to drive all the way to Brighton and back.

Usually when I magicked myself somewhere, it was back and forth between the human and sup worlds, or it was relatively short distances in Candlefield. This was a much bigger ask. To do it, I had to bring up a map on screen, so that I could get an idea of exactly how far I needed to travel, and where I wanted to end up.

I was all set. If it worked as planned, I would land in a quiet alleyway just off the promenade. Here goes nothing.

"What the—?"

Great! That worked out just swell. My calculations must have been slightly off because I ended up just beyond the beach, in the English Channel. Fortunately, the water only came up to my calves, so I was able to paddle back up to dry land.

"You should have taken your shoes off." A young boy making sandcastles shared those words of wisdom with me.

The well-dressed woman, behind the reception desk in the Lexicon, gave me a puzzled look as I squelched my way towards her.

"Good afternoon, *Madam*. Can I help?"

"I'd like to see the manager, please."

"What's it in connection with?"

"I'm—" At this point I deliberately mumbled the words, 'working with', then reverted to my normal voice. "The police."

"Police?" She looked doubtful, but said, "I'll go and get him. Please take a seat over there."

A few minutes later, she returned with a tall man in tow. He was smartly dressed, and was wearing shoes which were so shiny that I could see my face in them.

"I'm Rupert Bales, the manager. Karen tells me that you're a police officer." He glanced down at my shoes which were dripping water all over the polished floor. "Could I see your credentials?"

"Credentials?"

"Yes, please."

"I just need to ask you a few questions."

"And I'll be happy to answer them after I've seen your ID."

"Of course." I handed him my business card.

"This says you're a private investigator. Why did you tell my receptionist that you were a police officer?"

"I said I was *working with* the police. She must have misunderstood."

"I'm going to have to ask you to leave."

"I only need you to—"

"Right now, or I will call the *real* police."

That had gone remarkably well. Perhaps it was the wet feet that had given me away?

No matter. I'd tried the polite approach. Now, it was time for a little magic.

An hour later, I had everything I needed. All it had taken was an 'invisible' spell; the rest had been easy. In fact, the only reason it had taken that long was because I'd had to sit for fifteen minutes with my feet in the sun. There would have been no point to being invisible if I had left a trail of wet footprints behind me.

While the receptionist had been busy with a customer, I'd sneaked into the room marked 'private'. That's where they kept all their CCTV equipment. I had become something of an expert with the old CCTV, and I soon found the coverage for the date in question. Then I slowed it down a little, and studied all the guests' faces as they came to the reception desk. Just as the time stamp skipped past the midday mark, I spotted them. Brendan Bowlings was checking in, and behind him was another familiar face: Sarah Weller—his secretary.

Eureka!

It now seemed clear that Bowlings had been having an affair with his secretary. Had he also staged his own disappearance? Did Sarah Weller plan to join him later? I intended to find out.

***

My return trip to Washbridge proved to be much more successful. Just as planned, I landed close to the car park where I'd left my car that morning.

Jen was on her driveway when I arrived home. I had a sneaking suspicion that she'd been waiting to catch me because she came racing over.

"Everything okay, Jen?"

"Yeah, fine. I just thought I'd say hello."

"I imagine you heard our new neighbour last night?"

"Yeah. It woke me and Blake. Who are they?"

"It's a young guy. He's a student at Washbridge College. He's assured me it was a one-off."

"Good." She hesitated, and I could tell she had something on her mind. "You remember the other day when we were talking about blogs and stuff?"

"Yeah?"

"I just thought I should make it clear that I don't blog."

"Okay."

"Just in case you thought I did. Because I don't."

"Right. Thanks for clearing that up."

"And in particular, I don't blog about magic. Or wizards."

"Okay."

"I thought it best to tell you."

"Right."

Oh boy.

***

"You cannot be serious!" Jack sat up in bed.

I was already awake.

If anything, the music coming from next door was even

louder than the night before.

"There are loads of them out here." Jack had beaten me to the window.

It was just after two in the morning.

"I'm not standing for this!" I grabbed a T-shirt.

"Wait, Jill! I don't want you going around there. It could turn nasty."

"Trust me, it will, when I get hold of that little worm."

"No, Jill. Let me handle this in the morning."

"What's wrong with now?"

"Drink will have been flowing. There's no way to reason with people when they're drunk. I'll go around there first thing in the morning, and read them the riot act."

"I still think I should—"

"Please, Jill. I am a police officer, remember?"

"Okay."

I made us a cup of tea, and we sat and watched some awful TV for the next hour and a half. When the music finally stopped, we managed to catch a little sleep. I'd obviously been too trusting of Mr Worms, but hopefully, Jack would set him straight.

Chapter 16

The next morning, true to his word, Jack went around to have it out with The Worm. I wanted to go with him, but Jack insisted I'd only make matters worse.

"How did it go?" I said when he got back.

"It's all sorted."

"What did The Worm say about last night's party?"

"Apparently, it was his best friend's birthday, and they'd planned to celebrate in the common room at college, but there was some kind of electrical problem. It was all kind of last minute, and he promised it won't happen again."

"He said there'd be no more parties?"

"Definitely no more."

"And you believe him?"

"Yes, and I think I'm a pretty good judge of character."

"I hope so because I'll be here by myself tonight, seeing as how you're gallivanting across the country."

"I'm not sure a two-day residential assertiveness course qualifies as 'gallivanting'."

"You should have been assertive, and told them you didn't want to go."

"Will you be okay here by yourself?"

"I think I'll manage. I'm a big girl."

"You should invite Kathy over."

"No thanks. I'm looking forward to a quiet night in on my lonesome."

***

I'd parked the car, and was on my way to the office when I remembered Winky's lottery ticket. I daren't forget to collect his winnings again, or I'd never hear the end of it. And besides, I stood to make an easy five hundred pounds on the deal. I called in at the first newsagent's I came to, and went straight to the counter.

"I'm here to collect a lottery win."

"Congratulations, madam."

"It's not actually mine, it's — err — I mean, yeah, thanks. It's five thousand pounds."

"Very nice. If you could let me have the ticket, I'll get it processed for you."

"Just a second." I was sure I'd put the ticket in the little pocket in my handbag, but it wasn't there. It must have fallen out, and be somewhere in the bottom of the bag. I moved aside to let other customers get to the counter while I began to search. Five minutes later, and there was no sign of it, so I emptied the contents of the bag onto the counter. Ten minutes later, and I still hadn't found it. The lottery ticket clearly wasn't in my bag.

"Problem?" The man behind the counter asked.

"Err — no. Everything is fine. It must be in my other bag." I put everything back into the bag, and made my way outside.

Where was that stupid ticket? I'd used the same handbag all week, so it had to be in there, but it wasn't.

Winky was going to kill me.

***

It was Jules' day off. Mrs V was looking decidedly green around the gills.

"Morning, Mrs V. Did you have a good day yesterday?" I already knew the answer.

"No, I didn't. I've never been so ill."

"Sea sickness?"

"It was blowing a gale out there. The boat was going up and down, up and down. I thought I was going to die."

"How was Armi?"

"He was perfectly fine. He even ate a meal with the crew."

"I don't imagine you could face it?"

"I just wanted to die. If he ever suggests another boat trip, I'll kill him."

"Did you get it?" Winky was waiting for me just inside the door to my office.

"What?"

"You know what. My lottery cash. You promised you'd get it this morning."

"And I did try, but the terminals in the shop were down. Some kind of network problem, apparently. But I did get you a tin of your favourite red salmon."

"You'll have to try again, later."

"Of course. No problem."

I couldn't for the life of me think how the ticket could have dropped out of my bag, but it must have. Maybe it was in the car. But what if I'd dropped it on the street? I had to find it, or Winky would never forgive me.

"Jill, there's a man to see you." Mrs V still looked quite ill. "He says he's a—" She put a hand over her mouth for a moment, but then continued. "A fisherman. He wants to talk to you about the Bowlings case."

"Okay, Mrs V. Send him in, will you?"

Poor Mrs V. The smell of salmon can't have helped.

"Is that old girl alright?" the man asked, after Mrs V had shown him in.

"She was out on a fishing boat yesterday, and she's still feeling the after-effects. Please do have a seat. Mrs V said you have some information about Brendan Bowlings? Sorry, I don't know your name."

"Tommy Brakes. I fish down at Wash Point several times a week. I've known Brendan for years. Some of the guys on the river told me you'd been asking questions. I was at the dentist when you came around — dodgy molar. I saw Brendan on the day he's meant to have disappeared."

"Was he okay? Did he speak to you?"

"He was cheesed off. Brendan always used to fish the same spot, and always did really well there. That was until they built that stupid factory. After that, he had to move. Anyway, that day, he hadn't caught a thing, and he told me he was going back to his old spot. I asked if he'd forgotten about the fence, but he said he knew a way to get inside."

"Did he say how?"

"No. He just walked off. I figured he was just letting off steam. I never thought any more about it until I heard he'd gone missing."

"Did you tell the police?"

"Yeah, but they didn't seem very interested."

"Okay, well thanks, Tommy, for coming in."

"I hope you find him. He owes me a box of maggots."

Under different circumstances, I might have found Tommy's information more interesting, but having seen the footage from the hotel's CCTV, I was now convinced that Brendan Bowlings had deliberately gone missing. To confirm my suspicions, I would need to talk to his secretary, Sarah Weller.

***

"How do I look, Jill?" Barry was studying his reflection in the mirror.

"You look fantastic." He ought to — I'd just spent the best part of an hour grooming him.

"I want to win those Barkies. Do you think I'll win, Jill? Do you?"

"You'll definitely be in with a good chance."

"Jill!" Aunt Lucy called me back, just as I was about to leave with Barry. "I think I might be able to get those starlight fairy wings for you."

"Really?"

"Don't count your chickens just yet, but I put a few feelers out, and I've had word back from someone who thinks they might be able to put their hands on five pairs. I'll keep you posted."

"Thanks."

"Do you both want to be in the photo?" The photographer asked. Terry Eyre was a tall wizard in his late forties.

"I don't know. What are other people doing?"

"The rules allow for either a photo of the dogs by themselves or with their owner. It's been pretty much fifty-fifty up until now."

"I think I'll let Barry pose solo. I don't want to get the blame if he doesn't win."

I had to hand it to Terry, he took his job extremely seriously, and was the consummate professional.

"Barry! Look to the right," Terry called. "A little higher. That's perfect. Now, let's try one with you looking straight at the camera. Say 'bones'. Marvellous."

The whole shoot took just under thirty minutes, after which Terry asked me to choose the photograph I wanted to submit to the competition.

"I think Barry should be the one to choose."

"Can I see?" Barry came bounding over. "I'm very handsome, aren't I?"

"You certainly are. Which one do you want to use?"

"It's a difficult choice."

"You're going to have to make your mind up quickly. I have work to do."

"Okay. Err—that one."

"Good choice," Terry said. "Would you like me to print it off for you?"

"Yes, please."

I paid Terry a king's ransom, and then walked Barry back to Aunt Lucy's.

"Do you think I'll win, Jill? Do you? I want a year's supply of Barkies."

"We'll have to wait and see. There'll be a lot of entries."

When I dropped Barry off, Aunt Lucy took the photograph from me. She'd agreed to drop my entry form and photograph into The Candle's offices.

***

It was time to pay another visit to Amy Rice. I knew she was going to be disappointed with what I had to tell her.

"So far, I have nothing concrete that leads me to believe your husband's death was anything other than a tragic accident. The only thing that is a little unusual is that Gordon says Douglas telephoned to tell him he couldn't make it in on that Sunday."

"I don't believe that. Why would Doug tell Gordon that he couldn't make it, but then go in anyway?"

"I don't know. I was hoping you might have some kind of explanation."

"I don't, but I do know there had been some friction between Doug and Gordon for a while."

"What kind of friction?"

"I don't know. I asked Doug, but he wouldn't say. He said it was nothing."

"Did they often fall out?"

"Not really."

"I went to see Jordan too. He seems a little down on his luck."

"Is he still living in that grotty bedsit?"

"Yeah. It's pretty awful."

"He only has himself to blame. He has a serious gambling problem. I don't blame Sandra for throwing him out. He wanted to sell the business, but Doug and Gordon wouldn't hear of it. The business can only be sold if all three brothers vote to do it."

"Couldn't the other two have bought Jordan's share?"

"They could, but they wouldn't because they knew he'd only gamble away the cash."

"Did that cause bad feeling?"

"From what Doug told me, Jordan wasn't very happy about it, but there was nothing he could do."

"I can continue to investigate, if you like, but I have to be honest with you. I think you'll be throwing good money after bad."

"I'd like you to continue, at least for a while. I'll never believe that Doug's death was an accident."

***

I'd checked my bag again, and I'd searched every inch of the car, but there was no sign of Winky's lottery ticket. Great! I had no option but to come clean with him. Maybe, he'd be understanding, and accept that it was just one of those things.

Some chance!

"What do you mean, you've lost it?" he screamed at me.

"I put it in the pocket inside my bag, but when I got to the shop to claim the prize, it had gone."

"Gone where?"

"If I knew that, it wouldn't be lost, would it?"

"You'd better draw the money out of your bank account, then!"

"I'm not giving you five thousand pounds of my own money."

"That's okay. I wouldn't expect you to."

Phew!

"I only need four thousand, five hundred. I'd already agreed to let you have ten per cent."

"I can't afford to give you that kind of money."

"How do you intend to compensate me, then?"

"I—err—I suppose I could give you more salmon."

"Red?"

"Obviously."

"Every day?"

"Okay."

"For the rest of my life?"

"I suppose so."

Chapter 17

I'd just put Winky's salmon into a bowl when Mrs V came bursting into my office. The green tinge had gone, but she looked upset about something.

"Mrs V? What's wrong?"

"There's a most peculiar man out there. Most peculiar indeed."

"Who is it?"

"He has the strangest name. A Mr Macabre."

Oh bum! "That's our new landlord."

"That's what he said, but I thought he was lying. I threatened to tie him up with a scarf if he didn't tell me who he really was."

It looked like we were off to a great start.

I grabbed the bowl of salmon while Winky was still eating.

"Hey! What do you think you're doing?" He tried to knock it out of my hand with his paw.

"Our new landlord is here. If he sees you, we'll be out on our ear. Get under the sofa now!"

He moaned and groaned, but did as I asked, which was just as well because the imposing figure of Mr Martin Macabre appeared in the doorway.

"I'm not accustomed to being kept waiting in my own properties."

"Come in, Mr Macabre, or should I call you Martin?"

"Mr Macabre will do fine."

"Okay."

Macabre's gaze was flitting back and forth around the room—hopefully, Winky would have the good sense to remain hidden.

"What's that?" Macabre barked.

"What's what?" Then I realised I was still holding the bowl of salmon.

"It's — err — it's — my lunch."

"A bowl of salmon?"

"Yes."

"Just salmon?"

I nodded.

"Isn't that rather unusual? Wouldn't you prefer it with a salad or on a sandwich?"

"No. I like it like this." I grabbed some with my fingers, and stuffed it into my mouth. "Yummy!"

It would be impossible to adequately describe the look on Macabre's face.

"I believe your previous landlord, Mr Whiteside, has informed you that I have purchased this property, among others."

"Yes. Zac called in the other day."

"I do things rather differently to Mr Whiteside. I believe the key to being a successful landlord is to ensure that each property has the optimum tenants."

"Optimum?"

"Precisely, and I'm sorry to inform you that a — err — ?" He glanced around the office. "Private investigator? Or whatever it is you do, doesn't really fit in with my plans. The gym next door, however, is more the kind of thing I'd like to see in here. I understand from the owners of I-Sweat that they are hoping to expand."

"Hold on a minute. Are you saying what I think you're saying?"

"I'm sure we'll be able to agree on some kind of compensation package."

"Compensation for what?"

"Having to move out before your lease is up."

"I'm sorry, but I have no intention of moving out of this office. I have a lease, and I intend to stay here until it ends, which if I remember correctly is another thirty years."

"Unless you break the terms of your lease."

"I'd never do that."

"We'll see." He stood up. "My lawyers specialise in checking the small print."

"Good for them."

"You may know them. I believe they used to be based in this building."

Oh no! Please tell me it isn't true.

"You can expect a call from my man over there: Gordon Armitage."

Oh bum!

I'd expected Winky to come rushing out as soon as Macabre left, but there was no sign of him, so I got down on all fours and looked under the sofa.

"Hey, lazybones. Don't you want this?"

That's when I spotted it. Tucked into the loose lining of the underside of the sofa, was a ticket. A lottery ticket, to be precise.

"Here! Give me that!" He tried to snatch it, but I was too quick for him.

"What's this, Winky?"

He shrugged.

"Why is your winning lottery ticket hidden under the sofa?"

"It wasn't hidden, and anyway, that isn't the winning ticket. That's an old one."

"You're lying. This is the right date, and I remember these numbers. You must have taken it out of my bag."

And then the penny dropped.

I went over to my computer, and brought up the lottery website.

"Just as I suspected. You didn't win at all. Not one of these numbers matches the winning line."

"I must have misheard the numbers." He shrugged, all innocent-like.

"You set this up! It was you who took the ticket out of my bag. When did you do it? Was it when I was in the outer office? And then you tried to make me believe that I'd lost your ticket, and your winnings. You are a conniving little—"

"It was just a ruse. I know you enjoy a joke."

"Do I look like I'm laughing?"

"Not on the surface, but underneath—"

"Not anywhere. I'm never going to trust you again." I went back to my desk.

"What about the salmon?"

"Can you whistle?"

"A little. Why?"

"You can whistle for it."

***

I had to get out of the office before my head exploded. Not only did I have the world's most devious cat, but my landlord wanted me out. And who had he recruited to help him with that? None other than my old adversary, Gordon Armitage. This day was just getting better and better.

I decided to drop in on Kathy at Ever. If she was having a bad day too, we could cry on each other's shoulder.

"You smell of salmon." Kathy screwed up her nose.

"I've just fed the cat."

"I'm glad you came down. I have some fantastic news!"

"I could do with some."

"Not for you. For me, Pete and Jack. I knew you wouldn't mind."

"I already have a pounding headache. Could you stop talking in riddles, and tell me what you're going on about?"

"I managed to get tickets to see 'We' in concert. I could only get three though, but I didn't think you were all that bothered. Are you okay with the three of us going without you? I know Pete and Jack are big fans."

Okay about it? I was ecstatic. "I suppose I'll have to be. I'll just stay home by myself. Don't worry about me."

Playing the martyr? Who? Me? Snigger.

"It looks like you've had a rough day," Kathy said.

"I have a new landlord, and he wants me out."

"He can't do anything about it, though, can he?"

"I hope not. It depends if he can prove I've broken the terms of my lease."

"The first thing you need to do is get rid of that manky cat."

"Winky isn't a—" Wait a minute. Why was I about to defend Winky? "You could adopt him."

"Me?" Kathy looked horrified.

"It would be good for the kids to have a pet. It would give them a sense of responsibility."

"If I wanted a pet for the kids, I'd get a goldfish or a gerbil. Not a one-eyed horror-show of a cat."

Oh, well. I tried. "Where's Grandma?"

"She hasn't come in today. She's still licking her wounds after the Chameleon Wool fiasco. It seems to have knocked her confidence."

"Grandma? Never."

"It's true. She's been much more subdued than usual. Not that I'm complaining."

Just then, a number of customers came into the shop, so I left Kathy to it. It was good news about the 'We' concert. I'd been dreading being dragged to that awful thing.

There was a queue at Betty's shop again, but somehow today the atmosphere seemed different. When I got closer, I realised that the people in the queue weren't waiting to make purchases. They were all demanding refunds.

Betty came outside. It appeared that she'd taken a leaf out of Grandma's book, and left her assistants to handle the complaints.

"What's going on, Betty?"

"Don't ask. It's a nightmare."

"I thought business was good because of that YouTube starlet."

"It was, until Viv Royal admitted that she'd been two-timing her boyfriend, Baz Tuck. He's another YouTube personality. All her fans have turned against her, so now no one wants crustacean jewellery, and they're all demanding refunds."

"That's tough on you"

"What makes it worse is that I've bought in lots more stock to keep pace with demand."

"Oh dear."

"I'd better get back inside to help, otherwise my staff will down tools and walk out."

"Bye, Betty."

At least I wasn't the only one having a lousy day.

***

I paid a visit to the Human World Society at Pixie Central College, but instead of trying to get the members to come out onto the playing field to speak to me, I shrank myself to pixie size.

There were fewer members than I'd expected at the meeting: just five including Barnaby Bandtime who ran the society.

"Can I help you?" Barnaby looked a little puzzled to see a miniature witch come through the door.

"My name is Jill Gooder. I'm a private investigator. I've been hired to investigate the disappearance of Robbie Riddle who I believe was a member of this society."

"So what if he was?"

That wasn't the response I'd expected. Why so hostile?

"I'm just covering all the angles. I take it you knew Robbie?"

"Yes. He came to most of the meetings."

"And I believe he had a particular interest in the human world."

"Duh! Why else would he be a member of this society?"

I was beginning to dislike this obnoxious little pleb.

"When was the last time you saw Robbie?"

"At the last meeting." Barnaby made a point of checking his watch. "Look, if you don't mind, I'd like to get our meeting started."

"Just one last question?"

"What?"

"Do you have any idea what has happened to Robbie Riddle?"

"No. How should I know? I don't know anything. Nothing at all."

The pixie doth protest too much, methinks.

What? Of course I know my Shakespeare. Cultured and well-read, that's me.

As I made my way to the door, another one of the pixies bumped into me—seemingly deliberately. What a charming bunch the Human World Society were.

***

When I got back to the house, there were cars parked all along the road, and there were a lot of people milling around next door. Although the music hadn't started yet, it was obvious that they were preparing for another party: the third in as many days.

Worms was sitting on his doorstep, sandwiched between two attractive young women.

"Hi, Jill."

"Can I have a word in private, please?"

"Anything you have to say, you can say in front of Cindy and Candy."

The two women giggled.

"Are you planning on having another party?"

"Yeah. Do you want to join us?"

"No. You told me the first one was a one-off. Then, this morning, you promised Jack that there would be no more."

"Yeah, well, about that." He laughed. "I lied."

The two women giggled again.

He continued, "I like parties, and I'm probably going to have one most nights." He stood up, so he was in my face. "What are you going to do about it?"

There were so many things I wanted to do to him right there, but most of them would have got me arrested, or dragged back to Candlefield by the rogue retrievers. I had to play this smart.

"I'm kind of surprised you would want to rent this house," I said.

"Why?"

"I assume you know its history?"

"What history?"

"There was a mass murder here. It was known as the cleaver murders at the time. Very gruesome business."

He hesitated for a moment, but then cracked a smile. "Do you think I'm stupid? Is that supposed to scare me off?"

"Not at all. Why do you think the woman who used to live here left so suddenly? And why did she put the house up for rental? No one was ever going to buy it. They say the place is still haunted by the victims. At night, they roam the house, screaming in agony."

"Nice try, Jill, but it isn't going to work. You'll just have to get used to a lot of late night paaarrttiieees!"

"Yeah!" The giggle-twins shouted.

Hmm? We'd see about that. I made a call to Mad.

"Hey, Jill. I'm glad you called. Nails has started to go to Toppers Anonymous, and on the strength of that, Mum has taken him back."

"That's great news."

"Yeah, but she's threatened to throw him out again, if he doesn't keep up the meetings. Anyway, I owe you one."

"Funny you should say that because I could do with your help tonight."

"If I can, I will."

Chapter 18

It was the next morning, and I'd had my first good night's sleep in three days.

"Are you leaving us, Worms?"

It was a redundant question because his car was already overflowing with boxes and cases.

"Why didn't you warn me?" he said.

"About what?"

"This house is possessed!"

"I did tell you yesterday about the cleaver murders."

"I thought you were joking."

"Why would I joke about something like that? Your party ended very early last night."

"Is there any wonder? Everyone was terrified out of their minds."

"Where will you go?"

"I don't care. Anywhere that isn't here. I'll sleep on the dorm floor, if I have to."

And with that, he jumped into the car and sped off.

Mad had really come through for me this time.

Blake must have been watching from across the road because he came over. "Has he moved out?"

"It seems like it."

"Thank goodness. Jen and I barely got any sleep the previous two nights. I thought they were going to have yet another party last night, but then suddenly, everyone left."

"Yeah. That was kind of weird, wasn't it?" I grinned.

"Why do I get the impression that you may have had a hand in that, Jill?"

***

I didn't think there was anything to be gained by speaking to Sarah Weller at her place of work. She was likely to be embarrassed by the information I'd uncovered about her relationship with Brendan Bowlings, and would probably have clammed up. Tracing her address had been a trivial matter. Fortunately, it wasn't far from where I lived — just the other side of the toll bridge.

"Sarah!" I called to her, as she was about to get into her car.

"Yes?" It took her a few seconds to register who I was. "What are you doing here?"

"I'd like a quiet word."

"Couldn't you have come to the office?"

"I think this may be something you'd rather not discuss where we can be overheard."

"What do you mean? What's it about?"

"Hotel Lexicon?"

I could practically see the blood drain from her face.

"I — err — don't know what — "

"It might speed things along if I tell you that I've seen the CCTV from the hotel's lobby."

"You'd better come inside." She led the way into the house.

"I know what you're thinking," she said, as soon as we were inside. "But it isn't anything sleazy."

"That's none of my business. My only interest is in finding Brendan Bowlings. If you and he have arranged to run away, and live somewhere together, that's none of my concern. I just need proof that he is alive and well."

"Live together? What gives you that idea?"

"For starters, there's the hotel, and then there's his credit card bill. It looks as though you've enjoyed a lot of nights out together: the theatre and restaurants. Surely, you're not going to try to deny you and he are having an affair."

"I hate that word, but yes, Brendan and I have been seeing each other for a long time."

"And you finally decided to take it to the next level?"

"No. Brendan would never leave Sheila. I've always known that. He loves me, but he loves his wife as well. It's not like he's ever led me on. He's always said he'd never leave her, and I'm okay with that."

"Are you telling me that his disappearance wasn't something you'd planned together?"

"That's precisely what I'm telling you. I have no idea where Brendan is. I think something terrible must have happened to him." The tears began to well up in her eyes.

Either Sarah Weller had just given an Oscar worthy performance, or she was telling the truth, and Bowlings' disappearance was as much of a mystery to her as it was to everyone else. I was inclined to think the latter was true.

***

When I arrived at work, someone was waiting for me in the outer office.

"I told this *gentleman* that you wouldn't be able to see him without an appointment, Jill, but he insisted on waiting." Mrs V didn't try to disguise her contempt.

"What do you want, Gordon?" I had been expecting a visit from my nemesis, Gordon Armitage, but I hadn't thought it would be so soon.

"I see the place could still do with a lick of paint." Armitage stood up. The man was smugness personified.

"I'm busy, Gordon."

"That must be a novelty for you. I only need a minute of your time, but I'd prefer to speak to you in private."

"You'd better come through." As soon as I'd said the words, I regretted it. What if Winky was sitting on my desk?

"This office is just as bad as I remember it." Armitage looked as though he had a bad smell under his nose.

Fortunately, Winky was nowhere to be seen. I'd just have to hope he didn't come out from under the sofa, in search of food.

"So what exactly is it you want, Gordon?"

"You will no doubt have heard that your new landlord, Martin Macabre, has employed the services of Armitage, Armitage, Armitage and Poole."

"He did mention it."

"And you'll be pleased to learn that I have personally decided to take on this matter."

"I'm thrilled."

"I realise that we have some history, but I'm a reasonable man, and I'm prepared to put that behind us."

Yeah right. "Say what you came to say, Gordon."

"I'm sure Martin will have made it clear that he has big plans for this property, and that those plans do not include you."

"He made that perfectly clear, and I made it equally clear that he would get me out of here over my dead body."

"It will only take one minor breach of your lease to have you thrown out."

"I seem to recall that you didn't have much luck the last

time you tried that."

That wiped the smile off his smarmy face.

"All the more reason I'm determined to succeed now."

"Good luck with that. Now, I'd like you to leave."

"As I was saying, I'm a reasonable man, and so is Martin. If you relinquish your lease by the end of the week, Martin is willing to pay you a generous figure by way of compensation."

"I'm not interested. Now, if you wouldn't mind?"

"Wouldn't you like to know the figure he has in mind?"

"Is it twenty million?"

"No, of course not."

"In that case, you're wasting my time. Now, I really must insist you leave."

"The offer is fifteen thousand pounds. Very generous, I'm sure you'll agree. But this offer will only be on the table until close of business tomorrow." He took out his business card, and put it on my desk. "Call me if you change your mind."

"I won't."

Armitage had no sooner left than Winky made an appearance. "You should take the money and run."

"When I want your advice, I'll ask for it."

"We could retire to a nice cottage in the countryside."

"You'd better pray I don't accept the offer because if I do, you'll be back in the cat rehoming centre."

"Ouch!" He clutched his heart. "You can be very hurtful sometimes. Why would you say something like that?"

"Let me think. Maybe because this week alone you have tried to con me over a lottery win, and a ghost cat."

"You just can't take a joke. That's your problem."

I was still seething about Gordon Armitage when Brent from I-Sweat turned up.

"If you're here to try to talk me into moving out so you can expand, you can do one!"

"Whoa! Steady on, Jill. The new landlord came to talk to us yesterday, to feel us out about expanding into here, but as soon as we realised that he was planning on trying to force you out, we told him we weren't interested."

"But when you first moved in, you tried to persuade me to move out."

"That was before we got to know you, and before we realised what an emotional attachment you have to this place. You have nothing to worry about from us."

"Not from you, maybe, but I can't say the same about Macabre and his solicitors. Anyway, I'm sorry for jumping to conclusions. What did you want?"

"I just wanted to give you this." He handed me a card. "We promised you free lifetime membership if you got rid of those guys."

"Thanks. I take it they haven't been back, then?"

"We haven't seen hide nor hair of them since the day you scared them away. What exactly did it say on that note you had us pass to them?"

"I'm sorry, but if I told you that, I'd be forced to kill you." I grinned. "I'm pleased everything is okay now."

"Almost everything."

"Oh? What's wrong now?"

"It's nothing really."

"Go on. You might as well tell me."

"We've noticed that every morning when we open up, things seem to have moved around since the previous evening. Nothing's been stolen—just moved."

"What kind of things?"

"Nothing major. Weights, towels, lots of little things."

"That's weird."

"It's got us baffled."

"If you need any more help, let me know."

"We will. We're just going to see what happens over the next few days."

"Okay. Thanks for the membership."

"Our pleasure, but we expect to see you make use of it."

Oh bum! I had no excuse now for not taking exercise.

***

My mobile phone rang. It was Amy Rice.

"Something's happened." She could barely get the words out. "I can't believe it—it doesn't seem possible."

"Slow down, Amy. What's happened?"

"They've arrested Gordon. He's been charged with Doug's murder."

I hadn't seen that one coming.

"Are you absolutely sure they've charged him? He isn't just helping with their enquiries?"

"I'm sure. What do you think I should do?"

"Just sit tight for now. Do you think it's possible that Gordon could have murdered your husband?"

"I would have said 'no', but I don't understand why Gordon would say that Doug had called him, and told him he wasn't going in. That has to be a lie."

"Okay, Amy. Try to take it easy. I'll see if I can get any more information."

That of course was going to be easier said than done. Leo Riley was unlikely to throw me a bone, so I'd probably have to resort to magic.

Mrs V came through to the office. "There's a Mr Cross on the phone. He'd like to speak to you. He says he's the solicitor for Gordon Rice."

"Put him through, would you."

"Ms Gooder?" The man's voice was all private school and rowing competitions.

"Speaking."

"My client, Gordon Rice, has requested I get in touch with you. He was arrested earlier today, and charged with the murder of his brother. A charge which he strongly denies. He has asked me to contact you because he would like to speak to you in person."

"I'd be happy to, but will that be possible?"

"Not today, but hopefully tomorrow."

"I should warn you that the Washbridge police, and Leo Riley in particular, are not big fans of mine."

"That's irrelevant. You will be accompanying me as part of the defence team. Provided you don't have a problem with that?"

"None at all."

"Good. In that case, I'll be in touch as soon as I know where and when."

I made a quick call to Amy to bring her up to date on developments, and promised I'd let her know what came of my visit to see Gordon.

"It sounds like you have a cold coming on," Winky said. He was on the window sill, staring out across the way.

"You could be right." I'd had a runny nose all morning. I reached into my coat pocket for a tissue. As I took it out, a small scrap of paper fell onto the floor. At first, I thought it was just rubbish, but then I realised there was something written on it.

Where could it have come from? Then I remembered how one of the pixies had bumped into me when I'd been leaving the Human World Society. He must have slipped it into my pocket. The note was concise and simply read:

If you want to know what happened to Robbie, check out BeHuman

A friend.

Who or what was BeHuman?

Chapter 19

I'd had a call from Aunt Lucy to tell me that she'd managed to get hold of the starlight fairy wings.

"There you go." She handed me what looked like a ring box. "Be very careful with them because they're extremely fragile."

"Thanks."

I was just about to open the lid when she grabbed my hand.

"Don't open it in here. The draught might lift them out of the box. Take them upstairs into my bedroom, and open the box over the bed. That way, if they do fall out, they'll land on a soft surface."

"Okay."

"I should warn you. Barry isn't very happy with life."

"Why not?"

"The winners of the competition were announced in The Candle this morning, and he didn't win."

"Oh dear."

"He hasn't taken it well, as you can imagine."

I knelt next to the bed, and very carefully lifted the lid on the tiny box. At first, I thought it was empty, but then I saw what looked like a few specks of dust.

"Do you have a magnifying glass, Aunt Lucy?" I shouted from the top of the stairs.

"There's one in the top drawer of my bedside cabinet. I used it earlier to look at the wings."

Under the magnifying glass, I could see them in all their glory. They really were very pretty—the pattern on each one was unique.

"I didn't win!"

Barry made me jump so much that I almost dropped the box.

"Never mind, boy. You can't win them all." I closed the box, and returned the magnifying glass to the drawer.

"But I wanted a year's supply of Barkies."

"I know you did. Look, why don't I take you to the park?"

"Now? I love the park."

"I know."

"I love to go for a walk. Can we go now? Can we? Please!"

"Yes. Come on. Let's go and see the ducks."

Barry soon forgot about the competition once we arrived at the park because Dolly was there with Babs; the two dogs took it in turns to chase one another.

"Wears you out just looking at them, doesn't it?" Dolly said.

"I don't know where they get the energy from. How's Dorothy doing? I take it she's still living in Washbridge?"

"She is. She's doing okay, but I know she misses Babs."

"She must miss you, too?"

"I'd like to think so." Dolly smiled. "She comes over every couple of weeks, and I go and visit her occasionally. What about you? How are you finding living out in the sticks?"

"I'd hardly call it 'the sticks'. Smallwash is only a short drive from the city. We both like it, but I could do without the toll bridge. How is your painting coming along?"

I felt I should ask, just to be polite. I'd witnessed Dolly's painting at first-hand. She was a dear, but an artist?

Definitely not. All of her paintings looked like they'd been done by a five-year old. It wasn't that they were abstract — they were just plain bad.

"It's going really well, actually." She smiled. "I've had a number of commissions recently."

"That's good." Not so much for the subjects of the paintings, though.

"But the most exciting news is that I have an exhibition of my work tomorrow."

"That really is exciting." To say nothing of scary.

"It's in your cousins' coffee shop."

"In Cuppy C?"

"That's right. You must come."

"Err — yeah. If I can make it." I made a point of checking my watch. "Is that the time? I must be getting back. Barry! Barry! Come here!"

***

"Pearl, Amber, I need a quick word."

The twins were moving the tables out of one section of the tea room.

"Sorry, Jill. We've got lots to do to prepare for tomorrow's exhibition." Pearl pointed to the assistant behind the counter. "Jasmine will serve you."

"I'm not here for something to eat or drink."

"That makes a change." Amber laughed.

"I wanted a word about the exhibition."

"There's been a lot of interest." Pearl stopped what she was doing. "You are coming, aren't you?"

"I think you should cancel it."

"Are you out of your mind?" Amber joined Pearl. "Why

would we do that?"

"Who is the artist you're going to be featuring?"

"Her name is Dolly."

"That's what I thought. Have you actually seen any of her work?"

"No, but we hear that she's really good."

"Who did you hear that from?"

They looked at one another.

Amber shrugged.

Pearl shook her head. "I don't remember. Does it matter?"

"I've seen her work. In fact, she did a portrait of me, and one of Kathy, Peter and the kids. She's terrible."

"You say that," Pearl said. "But what do you know about art? I mean, really?"

"I know when someone can't paint for toffee."

"People say that about some of the most famous artists. You obviously don't have an eye for it, Jill. It's not your fault. You're more the practical sort."

"It has nothing to do with *having an eye for it*. I love Dolly to bits, but you have to believe me when I tell you — the exhibition will be a disaster. You have to cancel it while you still have time."

"We're not going to cancel." Amber scoffed at the idea. "We haven't had as much interest in anything since the Adrenaline Boys performed here."

"Don't you remember what a disaster the Sweaty Boys turned out to be?"

"That was a bad fit." Pearl conceded. "The exhibition is different. We're targeting a more upmarket audience."

"You mean like you did with the brochures that you had printed? Remind me again how that went?"

"They weren't as successful as we'd hoped," Amber said. "But this is different. This will get the more refined customers through the door."

Oh, well. No one could say I didn't try to warn them.

***

Timothy Troll had given me his address, and told me that he was usually home after his shift down the well finished at four pm. It was four-thirty so I was hoping to catch him.

All the houses on Troll Crescent had the same bizarre layout. Instead of having the door on the ground floor, it was in the roof. The only way to access it was via a steel staircase which ran up the side of the house.

"Hello?" He answered the door wearing PJs. "Oh, it's you. The book hooligan."

"I've apologised for that. Were you about to go to bed?"

"At this time of day? Of course not."

"You're wearing pyjamas."

"They're the most comfortable thing I own. I like to relax after I've finished work for the day."

"If you don't mind my asking, what exactly do you do down that well?"

"There are a million and one things to do, and it's not made any easier when *some* people drop their rubbish down it."

"I've got the starlight fairy wings you asked for."

His face lit up. "Where are they?"

"First things, first. I'd like to see the book."

"It might take me a few minutes to put my hand on it."

"I can wait."

He sighed. "Okay."

I'd expected him to ask me inside, but instead, he closed the door in my face.

Ten minutes later, there was still no sign of him, and I was about to knock again when the door opened. "I've found it," he said. "It was under the sledge."

"Someone threw a sledge down your well?"

"I told you. It's a very dangerous job."

I held out my hand for the book.

"Not so fast. The fairy wings, first."

I passed him the box. "Be careful. They're fragile."

"Please! I'm a collector. I think I know how to handle them."

"Sorry."

He took a jeweller's eye-glass out of his pocket, had a quick peek inside the box, and then nodded his approval. "Excellent. Here's your book. Please be more careful with it in future."

***

Now that I had Magna Mondale's book, I would be able to claim the journal that Imelda Barrowtop had left to me in her Will. I called her solicitor, but he was unable to see me for a couple of days. That journal had better contain something interesting, after all the trouble I'd had to go to in order to claim it.

There was another reason I'd wanted to get Magna's book back. On her deathbed, Imelda Barrowtop had mistaken me for Magna Mondale, and had asked if I'd completed the 'double dark' spell. To placate her, I'd told her that I had, but I was now curious to find out what that spell was all about. Although I'd studied the book during the short period of time it had been in my possession, I didn't recall seeing that particular spell. I wasn't sure if I'd just missed it the first time around, or if it wasn't actually in the book. Jack wouldn't be back from his course until late, so I'd be able to study the book once I got back to the house.

I'd just arrived home when Megan and her boyfriend, Ryan, pulled up in his car. She looked so much better than she had the last two times I'd seen her. As soon as she spotted me, she grabbed Ryan's hand, and led him over. I was pleased to see that she was wearing a scoop neck T-shirt, and that there were no more bruises on her neck.

"Jill!" She was back to her bubbly self. "This is Ryan."

Ryan and I exchanged a conspiratorial smile.

"Nice to meet you, Ryan." I shook his hand.

"I'm making dinner for him," she said. "I've told him not to expect too much."

"I'm sure it will be great. I'm eating alone tonight because Jack is away on a course."

"You can join us if you like, Jill. Can't she, Ryan?"

"Sure. The more the merrier."

"That's very kind of you both, but I have things I need to do. You two have a great evening."

When I turned back to watch them go into her house, Ryan gave me a quick thumb's up.

***

As soon as I'd grabbed a snack, I began to study Magna's book. The spells, although very advanced, no longer left me in awe. I had Magna to thank for my initial advancement, but I now felt I'd taken my skills to an even higher level.

After an hour with no success, I was beginning to think there was no such thing as the 'double dark' spell. Imelda Barrowtop had been delirious when she'd asked me about it—maybe it had been a figment of her imagination? But then I spotted a spell at the very back of the book. I'd missed it the first time I'd looked through the book because there were several blank pages in front of it. The title of the spell simply read: DD.

That had to be it.

I spent the next twenty minutes studying it, but was no wiser when I'd finished. It was by far and away the most complicated and advanced spell I'd ever come across. I was usually able to analyse any spell in order to work out what it did, but I had no clue what this one was supposed to do. It was so frustrating. What good was finding the spell if I didn't know what it did? My only option was to cast the spell, to see what happened, but that was fraught with danger. It could do absolutely anything.

I put the book to one side, and switched on the TV. Maybe that would take my mind off it.

Thirty minutes later, I switched it off again. It was no good—I couldn't put the 'double dark' spell out of my mind. I was going to risk it—I was going to cast the spell. After a quick refresher, I focussed as hard as I could, and then went for it.

Nothing happened. At least nothing I could see, but I did feel an incredible energy flow through my body. It wasn't painful, but it sure was weird. In the end, I came to the conclusion that the 'double dark' spell must have been a work-in-progress. It was beginning to look like I'd never know what Magna had intended the spell to do.

Jack would be home soon, so I took the book out to the car and put it in the boot.

"How was your course?" I asked when he arrived, just after eight o' clock.

"On a scale of nought to boring, it was tedious beyond belief."

"Can I expect you to be more assertive towards me now?"

"Would you like me to be?"

"I don't know. It might be fun."

"You'll have to wait a while to find out. I need something to eat first. I'm starving."

"You old romantic, you."

"Did you have any problems with 'The Worm' last night?"

"None at all."

"My talk with him obviously did the trick."

"Obviously. In fact, we won't be getting any more problems from next door from now on."

"How can you be so sure?"

"The Worm has moved out."

"How come? He's only just moved in."

"You must have scared him to death."

"I guess so. I can be quite intimidating at times."

I laughed.

"What's so amusing?"

"The thought of you being intimidating."

"Cheek." He started for the stairs, but then remembered something. "Hey, have you heard about the concert?"

"You mean the 'We' concert? The one that I don't have a ticket for? The one that you, Kathy and Peter are going to while I stay at home?"

"Now, I feel bad about it."

"You mustn't. That was never my intention." Snigger.

"Maybe we'll be able to pick one up for you from one of those websites where they resell tickets?"

"No, it's okay. I'll manage to amuse myself somehow."

"Are you sure?"

"Yes. Don't worry about me sitting at home all alone. I'll be perfectly fine."

Chapter 20

It was the next morning, and Jack was just about to leave for work.

"I wonder who our new neighbour will be," he said.

"Whoever it is, they can't be any worse than Worm."

"That's true. By the way, I meant to mention, I saw Megan's new boyfriend yesterday."

"So did I. She was going to make him dinner, apparently."

"Lucky guy."

"Hey, I take my turn at making dinner."

"You have a funny idea of how 'turns' work, Jill."

"I don't know what you mean."

"Take last week. I made dinner on Monday, Wednesday and Friday."

"And I made it on Tuesday and Thursday."

"Spot anything wrong there?"

"No."

"Monday, Wednesday and Friday makes three days. Tuesday and Thursday makes two days."

"Yeah, but what about the weekends?"

"We usually eat out at the weekend."

"It evens itself out over a period of weeks."

"It would do, except that at the beginning of every week you always say: *It's Monday – it's your turn to make dinner*."

"I never say that." I so did.

"So, you'll make dinner next Monday, will you?"

"Sure. No big deal."

"Okay. I'm off. See you tonight."

That wasn't good. Jack was catching on to all my cunning plans.

My phone rang, and it was just the person I wanted to hear from at that time of the morning. Not!

"Good morning, Grandma."

"It certainly isn't a *good* morning."

Here we go. "What's wrong?"

"You may well ask."

I waited for an answer, but instead got radio silence. "Hello?"

"I'm too angry to speak." She sounded it too.

"What's wrong?"

"I don't have time to tell you right now because I have to recalibrate the Chameleon Wool. Pop around to Ever later this morning."

"Okay, but it might help if I knew what—"

She'd hung up.

Well, that was something to look forward to.

***

I'd decided that my new keep-fit regime would start that day, so instead of going straight into the office, I went to I-Sweat. Now I had lifetime membership, I no longer had an excuse for not making regular visits to the gym.

The place was heaving. I'd assumed that early mornings would be a quiet time, but I'd got that wrong. I had to wait to get on a treadmill.

"Morning, Jill." It was George—one of the owners. "I was beginning to wonder if we'd ever see you in here."

"The free life membership helped to make my mind up. I didn't think it would be this busy though."

"A lot of people like to get in a session before work. It sets them up for the day. We stay open late two days each week: Monday and Friday. It's a lot quieter then. Most people are too bushed after a day at work to think about going to the gym. Maybe one of those sessions would be better for you?"

"Are you trying to say that I don't work very hard?"

"No, that's—err—not—"

"It's okay. I'm only joking. I might check out those late night sessions."

"You're rather red in the face, Jill," Jules greeted me.

"I've just been working out, next door."

"You should take it easy."

"If you say, 'at your age', you'll be back at the black pudding factory."

She grinned. "Annabel isn't coming in today."

"She's not on the high seas again, is she?"

"No. I doubt she'll do that again in a hurry. She rang in to say her sister was coming up."

"Mrs G? Oh dear. That's not good news."

"Have you met her sister, then?"

"Oh yes. She's a nightmare. She spends all of her time putting Mrs V down."

"I'm surprised Annabel stands for that. She usually doesn't take any—"

"I know, but Mrs G seems to be her Achilles heel. By the way, how is Gilbert doing in his new job?"

"He loves it, and the money is much better than he's been used to. He must be feeling flush because he's taken up a new hobby." Jules pulled a face.

"I take it you don't approve?"

"It's just a bit weird. I've never heard of anyone collecting them before."

"Collecting what?"

"Bottle tops."

I laughed.

"See, I told you it was weird. Why can't he collect coins or stamps like everyone else?"

"I wouldn't worry about it. There are more toppers than you might think."

"How do you know the lingo?"

"I know far more about the mysterious world of bottle tops than I ever wanted to."

Winky totally ignored me when I walked into the office. He was fiddling with something, and he seemed totally mesmerised by whatever it was.

"What are you up to, Winky?"

"Here, this is for you." He handed me a paper swan.

"Origami?"

"Do you like it?"

"It's very good." To be fair, he'd made an excellent job of it. "I didn't realise you were into origami."

"You're looking at an origami master."

I should have known. "How come I've never seen you do it before?"

"What can I say? I like to keep my light firmly secreted under a bushel."

Yeah, right. "Do you do requests?"

"Of course. What would you like me to make for you?"

"How about a flower?"

"You need to be more precise. A tulip? A rose?"

"A rose, please."

"Your wish is my command." He picked up a blank sheet

of paper, and began to fold it, this way and then that. Moments later, he handed me a beautiful paper rose.

"That's brilliant, Winky. Honestly, I'm really impressed."

"I find it gives me a sense of Zen."

Just when I thought that cat couldn't surprise me ever again, he did. And for once, not in a bad way.

***

I'd arranged to meet with Crispin Cross, Gordon Rice's solicitor, at Washbridge police station. I arrived first, and was waiting in reception when my old friend, Leo Riley, came walking through.

"Gooder? What are you doing here?"

"Nice to see you too, Leo."

"It's Detective Riley to you. I asked why you were here?"

"I'm on the defence team for Gordon Rice."

"Don't make me laugh." He scoffed. "You won't be seeing anyone."

"That's where you are wrong, Detective." Crispin Cross appeared at my side. "Ms Gooder is with me." He took out a manila folder, and extracted two sheets of paper, which he handed to Riley. "I'm sure you will find all the paperwork in order."

Riley's face transitioned through several shades of red, as he studied the papers.

"I'm not happy about this," he pronounced, after he'd handed back the file.

"That's as it maybe, Detective." It was obvious that Cross wasn't intimidated by Riley. "Nonetheless, I'd be grateful if you would take us to our client."

Fifteen minutes later, we were shown into an interview room where Gordon Rice was waiting for us.

"I didn't kill Doug!"

"Please, Gordon." Cross held up his hand. "You must try to remain calm."

"Sorry."

"You asked me to bring Ms Gooder here today."

Rice looked to me. "I didn't know who else to turn to. The police have decided I'm guilty. I know you're already investigating Doug's death for Amy. I thought maybe you could help to clear my name?"

"I certainly intend to find out what really happened."

"That's all I ask."

"Why did the police arrest you. Do you know?"

"They've checked my phone log, and they say there was no record of a phone call from Doug. But I know what I heard. He called me to say he couldn't make it in."

"Is that all they have on you?"

"I wish it was." He hesitated. "They have CCTV of me on that day."

"CCTV from your factory?"

"No, we don't have it installed. They have footage from the car park of a restaurant, half a mile up the road, and from the petrol station opposite our unit."

"What does the CCTV show?"

"I haven't actually seen it yet, but they say it shows me arriving at, and then later, leaving the restaurant."

"Are you denying that it was you on the tape?"

"I did go to the restaurant, so they may well have caught me on CCTV there. But they claim they also have footage of me entering our unit in between the time I was seen arriving at, and leaving the restaurant. They think I sneaked out, and went down to the factory."

"Were you with anyone at the restaurant who can vouch for the fact that you didn't leave there?"

He hesitated. "No."

"Did you eat alone?"

He hesitated again.

"Gordon, you have to tell me if you want me to help you."

"I can't. And what does it matter, anyway? I didn't do it. I didn't murder Doug."

Despite our best efforts, neither I nor Cross could get Gordon to tell us who he had been with at the restaurant.

"What's wrong with him?" I said, once we were outside the police station. "Doesn't he know he could go down for this if he doesn't tell us who he was with?"

"Clients are strange creatures, Ms Gooder. That's one thing I've learned over the years."

***

My next stop was Ever A Wool Moment, to find out what Grandma was so het up about.

Chloe was behind the counter.

"Hi, Jill."

"No Kathy?"

"She's on a day's holiday. She said she was going shopping for clothes for a party."

The golden wedding. I might have known. Kathy didn't need much of an excuse to add to her wardrobe.

"My grandmother is expecting me."

"She's in the office."

Grandma was muttering to herself while sticking large needles into something.

"Good morning, Grandma."

"What's good about it? Sit down, we have important business to discuss." She placed the object, which looked like some kind of voodoo doll, onto her desk.

"Who's that meant to be?"

"Dominic Duxberry. The leader of the Combined Sup Council."

"What has he done to upset you?"

"That's why I asked you to come over. I take it you haven't heard, then?"

"Heard what?"

"There's a rumour that the council are going to try to pass a new regulation, which would mean that sups living in the human world will have to pay taxes on the money they earn there."

"That can't be right. We already pay taxes in the human world."

"Is that so? Well thank you for enlightening me. I had no idea." The wart on the end of her nose was throbbing red. "Why do you think I'm so angry?"

"It will affect me too."

"You? I don't know why *you're* worried. Based on how little business you have, they'll owe you money."

Harsh. But probably true.

"It will cost me a small fortune!" Grandma yelled. "If they think I'm going to take this lying down, they have another think coming."

"What do you intend to do about it?"

"*You* are going to stop the motion being carried by the

council."

"Me? I'm only one vote. How am I meant to defeat the motion by myself?"

"That's your problem. You can't expect me to have all the answers."

Great!

**

I wanted to follow up on the note that had been slipped into my pocket by one of the pixies at the Human World Society. I could have tried the police to see if they'd let me see their files on the other missing pixies, but Maxine Jewell was unlikely to give me the time of day. Instead, I called in at Candlefield Library, and began a search of the archives.

Generally speaking, I enjoyed living in the human and sup worlds equally, but there was one major exception.

Having no internet was a real pain when it came to research. It didn't help that the library service didn't bother to archive newspapers onto microfiche. Instead, I had to search through the physical copies that were stored in the basement. It was a thankless job, and the dust didn't help — it got everywhere.

"Achoo! Achoo!"

"Are you okay?" The librarian enquired when I eventually re-emerged from the basement. Her ensemble today consisted of a paisley-patterned two-piece with matching walking stick. Nice!

"Yeah. Achoo! It's just the dust."

"Did you find what you were looking for?"

"I think so. Thanks."

Surprisingly, the search for articles on the other missing

pixies had proven to be easier and more productive than I'd expected. In the last three months, two other pixies had been reported as having gone missing. In both cases, it was obvious the articles had only been written because relatives or friends had approached the newspaper — presumably in the hope that the publicity might help to find their loved ones. Neither article suggested there had been any police involvement.

I had less joy searching for information on BeHuman — I drew a complete blank.

Chapter 21

I wanted to take a look at the CCTV from both the restaurant and the petrol station, so I planned to give them the usual *'I'm working with the police'* routine.

Fortunately for me, the restaurant manager took me at my word, and didn't ask to see my credentials. He was more than happy to show me through to the office where the CCTV was monitored.

"Do you need any assistance?" The helpful manager offered.

"No, thanks. I know my way around these systems. You can leave me to it."

"Okay. What about something to eat or drink?"

"That would be nice."

"I'll get you one of our bar menus. On the house, of course."

"That's very kind."

"We're always happy to help the police."

If Leo Riley ever found out what I'd been up to, I'd be all kinds of dead.

I didn't want to take too many liberties, so I settled for sandwiches, a bowl of chips and a lemonade. I'd no idea what time of day Gordon Rice had visited the restaurant, so I was forced to watch the CCTV from the time the restaurant opened. I set the recording to fast forward, but not so fast that I might miss something. It made for tedious viewing, but I had to maintain my concentration.

During the first hour or so of the recording, there was very little activity. Things started to pick up as lunchtime approached. I had to keep my wits about me to make sure

I checked all the customers as they arrived and left. When the time-stamp showed two-thirty, the level of activity dropped off once again.

"Can I get you another drink?" The manager was back to check on my well-being.

"A cup of tea would be nice."

"Milk and sugar?"

"Milk and one and two-thirds spoonfuls of sugar, please."

He'd obviously been well trained in the hospitality industry because he didn't even blink at my exacting sugar requirements.

"Would you like anything with that? We have some delicious cakes."

"Anything chocolatey?"

"I'm sure I can find something."

I was beginning to enjoy this.

The slice of chocolate cake was delicious, and enormous, but somehow I managed to finish it.

The action on the CCTV had slowed down considerably. No one had arrived in the car park for the previous twenty minutes, but then a blue Fiat car pulled up. Was that Gordon? I had no idea what kind of car he drove. Nope. It was a woman. Five minutes later, a red Peugeot arrived. This time it was Gordon Rice who disappeared into the restaurant. From what Gordon had told me, the police believed that he had sneaked out the back door, gone to the factory, killed his brother, and then returned to the restaurant. There was no CCTV coverage at the back of the building, so there was no proof that he'd ever left the restaurant. The evidence was purely circumstantial, but it didn't help his case that he had apparently lied about the phone call he'd received from Douglas. I continued to watch the screen—waiting for Gordon to leave. About ninety minutes further into the recording, the woman in the blue Fiat left. A few minutes later, Gordon drove away. I thanked the restaurant manager for his hospitality, and then took my leave.

The petrol station manager wasn't as convivial. He moaned and groaned that he'd already been through this once, but he allowed me to view the footage anyway. It was much easier this time because I was now aware of the time-frame during which Gordon was supposed to have sneaked out of the restaurant. Sure enough, roughly twenty minutes after the time I'd seen footage of him parking his car in the restaurant car park, a figure came into frame, and disappeared into the unit. The quality of the CCTV wasn't great, and the figure never faced the camera, but it certainly appeared to be Gordon Rice.

The CCTV set-up at the petrol station was fairly basic, and had very little by way of security. I hadn't been able to take a copy of the restaurant's CCTV, but with this set-up, I was able to 'cut out' the clip I needed, and email it to my phone. At least now, if I needed to view it again, I could do so without having to go all the way back to the petrol station.

I felt this case was getting away from me a little, but there was still one more person I wanted to talk to, and that was Jordan Rice's wife, Sandra.

***

I'd promised to attend the first art exhibition to be held at Cuppy C, but in all honesty, I would much rather have given it a miss because it was bound to be an unmitigated disaster. I'd tried my best to warn the twins about Dolly, but they had dismissed my concerns out of hand—as usual.

As I approached the shop, I expected to hear the sound of raucous laughter, as everyone poked fun at Dolly's 'masterpieces', but instead, there was barely a sound coming from inside. Maybe everyone had already left in disgust at having been brought there under false pretences?

I took a deep breath, and stepped inside the shop.

Far from being empty, Cuppy C was heaving with people, and many of them were not regulars. Judging by the way they were dressed, these were the upper-class punters that the twins had been hoping to attract. What was even more surprising was the fact that everyone seemed to be enthralled by the paintings.

"Her use of colour is exquisite," a woman wearing a bird's nest hat said.

"The paintings speak to my very soul," a man with a monocle commented.

And on and on it went. Everywhere I looked, people were discussing Dolly's paintings. And no one was laughing.

"What did we tell you, Jill?" Pearl appeared behind me. "It's a roaring success."

"How?" I whispered. "Look at these things. They're awful."

Amber joined us. "Have you ever considered that you're not cultured enough to appreciate such works of art, Jill?"

I ushered them behind the counter, and through to the stairs where we could speak more freely.

"You two are having a laugh, aren't you?"

"What do you mean?" Pearl said.

"You know these paintings are rubbish. You're just encouraging that crowd out there to go along with the 'Emperor's New Clothes' charade."

"You just can't admit you're wrong, can you?" Amber said. "Everyone thinks Dolly's paintings are masterpieces. Everyone except you."

"They're not masterpieces. They are complete—"

Just then, the artist herself joined us.

"err—complete—err—completely fantastic," I said. "I love them, Dolly."

What? Who are you calling two-faced?

"Thank you, Jill. I never dreamed it would go as well as this. I've already sold four paintings."

"It's no more than you deserve," I heard myself say.

After Dolly had gone back into the shop, the twins both gave me a look. I couldn't be sure if it was disbelief or disapproval—probably both.

The exhibition was still in full swing when I made my excuses and left.

It was now official. I knew nothing whatsoever about art.

***

I'd arranged to visit Rhoda Riddle's house to bring her up to date on her son's disappearance. She'd asked if Maddy and Lionel could join us, and I'd said that was a good idea. Rather than have to conduct the meeting outdoors, I once again shrank myself to pixie size so I could get into the house. Rhoda gave us all a cup of pixie tea, which I'd never tried before. It was delicious.

We were seated around an oval shaped dining table.

"I'll be honest with you, Rhoda," I said. "I'm no closer to

finding Robbie, but I do have a couple of leads I'm still working on."

"What kind of leads?"

"Well, for a start, I now know that Robbie isn't the only pixie to have gone missing in recent weeks."

"I'd heard rumours that was the case, but I didn't believe it," Rhoda said. "Surely, if that was true, the police would have investigated?"

"They should have, but the truth is that they're not treating any of the disappearances as suspicious. They believe Robbie and the others left of their own free will. That might be okay if it was a single disappearance, but there really is no excuse for them not to take it more seriously now that three pixies are missing."

"Do you think I should go back to the police?"

"It can't do any harm, but it probably won't do much good either. My impression of the Candlefield police to-date has been less than favourable."

"You said you had a *couple* of leads," Maddy said.

"Yes. While I was at Pixie Central College, someone slipped a note into my pocket suggesting I check out something called BeHuman. I don't know who or what it is, but it's possible they may have something to do with the disappearances. The problem is, so far, I haven't been able to find any information about them. I'm not sure they even exist."

"Robbie mentioned them to me," Lionel said.

"He did? When?"

"A few weeks ago. You know what Robbie is like." Lionel turned to Maddy. "He's always rattling on about the human world. He'd just come from one of those meetings of his."

"The Human World Society?" I suggested.

"Yeah. That was it. To be honest, I got fed up of listening to him going on about it. Anyway, he mentioned a company which he reckoned was going to change everything."

"Change everything how?"

"I've no idea. I'd totally switched off by then. He did give me a leaflet, though. I just shoved it in my pocket."

"Do you still have it?"

"I think so. It's in the pocket of my jacket, back at my place."

"In that case, Rhoda and Maddy, you stay here. I'll go with you, Lionel. I want to see this leaflet."

For a little guy, Lionel walked at one heck of a pace. By the time we reached his place, I was out of breath. So much for my new fitness regime.

"Are you okay, Jill?" Lionel asked. "You're really red in the face."

"Me?" I gasped. "I'm fine. I must have put on a little too much blusher this morning. That's all."

Lionel found the crumpled leaflet in his jacket pocket, and passed it to me: 'BeHuman – *The Human Experience For Pixies.*' Below that was a phone number.

"Do you think it could be important?" Lionel said.

"Whoever put the note in my pocket at the Human World Society obviously did, and it's not as though I have any better leads. I think I should get in touch with them."

"I see one slight problem with that, Jill. You're not a pixie."

"That's true, but the 'size' thing isn't a problem. Do you

think I could pass as a pixie — with a bit of work?"

"Maybe, with *a lot* of work."

"Okay. I'll give them a call."

***

I tried the number on the leaflet, but there was no reply — not even an answerphone. I told Lionel that I'd give it another try the following day, but if that didn't work out, I'd probably have to admit defeat. I was beginning to hate 'missing person' cases. I'd got nowhere trying to locate Brendan Bowlings, and now I'd drawn a blank trying to find Robbie Riddle.

I was such a super sleuth. Not!

After I'd magicked myself back to Washbridge, I picked up the car and was on my way home. As I drove past my office building, I noticed that there were lights on in I-Sweat. I thought that strange because it wasn't one of their late opening nights. I might have dismissed it, but I remembered what George had said about things being mysteriously moved around during the night. I could have pretended I hadn't seen anything; no one would ever have known. After all, I'd had a lousy day, and all I really wanted to do was get home, and dive into a packet of custard creams.

But it was no good. I'd never forgive myself if I ignored it, and then found out in the morning that the I-Sweat guys had been burgled.

After I'd parked the car, I made my way up to the gym. The doors were locked, and I could see through the glass that the reception area was in darkness. But beyond that, there were lights on in the gym. I needed to get a look inside, and I knew just how I could do it. I hurried down to my offices, which were in darkness, and let myself in. Fortunately, Winky was nowhere to be seen when I made my way across my office to the window. He was no doubt curled up asleep under the sofa. After climbing onto the ledge, I cast the 'levitate' spell, and then floated around the outside of the building, until I came upon the windows which looked into I-Sweat.

"What the—?"

The sight that met me was so shocking that I almost lost focus, and plummeted to the ground. The gym was doing a roaring trade; almost every piece of equipment was in use. And yet, there wasn't a single human to be seen—the gym was full of cats. I'd been wrong about Winky. He wasn't under the sofa in my office. He was standing at the far side of the gym, talking to a couple of female cats. It was all beginning to make sense: The leaflets that I'd seen for the Moonlight Gym, and the casual way that Winky had denied that he would be using my office as a gym.

How long had this been going on? How much money was Winky making on the deal? And how were the cats getting into the gym when the main doors were locked?

There was no point in making a scene there and then, but I'd be having a few choice words with my darling cat in the morning.

Chapter 22

The next morning when I came down for breakfast, Jack was in full-blown panic mode.

"We haven't got them a present!" he said. "I've been so busy thinking about who's going to the party that I totally forgot we need to buy them a present."

"So, we'll get them one."

"That's easy for you to say, but what?"

"I don't know. How about a subscription to Netflix?"

"Netflix?" He gave me that look of his.

"What's wrong with Netflix?"

"There's nothing wrong with it, but do you really think it would be an appropriate gift for a golden wedding anniversary?"

"I don't see why not."

"The whole point is that you buy something golden."

"Says who?"

"It's the rules."

"No, it isn't. On Kathy and Peter's fifth wedding anniversary, I didn't give them a plank of wood. I bought them a year's supply of custard creams."

"Sadly, I believe you. First off, that is a really dumb present."

"Thanks."

"And secondly, I bet you ended up eating most of them."

That much was true, but I wasn't about to admit to it.

"Okay. If you want to get them something golden, go for it. What did you have in mind?"

"I was thinking maybe a condiment set."

"Gold salt and pepper pots?"

"What do you think?"

"Sure, why not? I bet they'd prefer the Netflix subscription, though."

***

It was Jules' day off.

"Good morning, Mrs V."

"It most certainly is not."

Maybe if I didn't ask, she wouldn't tell me why.

"And, I'll tell you why." She sighed. "G wants to move to Washbridge."

"That's not good."

"You haven't heard the half of it. She says that we should live together, so that we can share our living costs."

"She wants to move in with you?"

"That's why she came over. She has it all planned out."

"Did she ask how you felt about the idea?"

"Of course she didn't. She just assumed I'd go along with it."

"Why don't you explain that you don't want her living with you?"

"How am I supposed to do that? You know what G is like. She doesn't listen to anyone—especially not me." Mrs V hesitated. "You have to help me, Jill."

"Me? What can I do?"

"You're always sorting other people's problems out. You're really good at it." That was true. "I know you'll be able to come up with something."

"I suppose I could give it some thought."

She stood up, came around the desk, and gave me a hug. "Thank you, Jill. I knew I could rely on you."

No pressure, then.

Before I could go through to my office, Mrs V remembered something else.

"You'll need to order some more copy paper, Jill. We're all out."

"Already? I only bought three reams a couple of weeks ago."

"It's all gone. I checked this morning."

"Okay."

Moments later, I discovered why we were out of paper. My office was full of origami models: animals, birds, flowers, to name but a few. Winky was on the sofa, churning out yet another swan—they were obviously his favourite.

"What's going on, Winky?"

"With what?"

"With all this origami?" I was trying to thread a path to my desk without stepping on any of the paper models.

"I thought you liked them?"

"I do, but that doesn't mean I want my office covered in them. You've used up all the copy paper."

"That reminds me. Can you order some more?"

"Not for you, I can't. If you want any more paper for your origami, you can buy some yourself."

"Where am I supposed to get the money from?"

"Hmm? Let me think. How about the money you made from the subscription fees for Moonlight Gym? Or should I say I-Sweat?"

His expression changed; he knew he'd been rumbled. "I don't know what you mean."

"I think you do. I saw you through the window last night."

"How did you get up there?"

"Have you forgotten that I'm a witch?"

"That's not playing fair."

"If we want to talk about *not playing fair*, how about we start by discussing the fact that you're selling subscriptions to someone else's gym?"

"What harm am I doing? It's not like anyone else uses the gym during those hours."

"How about the cost of the electricity you're burning, or the wear and tear on the equipment?"

"Now you're just nit-picking."

"I doubt the owners would agree. They think that someone has been breaking in."

"How do they know? Did you tell them?"

"No. They could tell some things had been moved."

"I suppose you're going to dob me in?"

"I should."

"What cut do you want to stay quiet?"

"I don't want a cut of your ill-gotten gains."

"What will keep you quiet, then?"

"Two things. Firstly, you have to have a serious talk to all of your members to make sure they tidy up after themselves, and put things back where they should be. If they don't, then I won't need to tell the owners, they'll set up their own surveillance."

"Agreed. What's the second thing?"

"It strikes me that your cat buddies must cover most of Washbridge. I need them to be my eyes and ears."

"For what?"

"Nothing specific, but I'd like them to be on call should I need them. For example, if a child went missing, you could get your posse to keep a lookout for them."

"Okay. I can organise that."

"Right then. We have a deal, but if the owners catch you, you're on your own. Oh, and one last thing. How do you get into the gym?"

"That would be telling." He grinned.

***

I tried the number for BeHuman again. This time, to my surprise, someone answered.

"Oh, hi," I said. "I'd like to book for the Human Experience."

"How did you get this number?"

If this was their idea of customer service, I wasn't impressed.

"I'm a member of the Human World Society at Pixie Central College."

"I see. Sorry, but we have to be careful. The Human Experience is not available to just anyone."

"I understand." I didn't really. None of this made much sense. "Could you give me any more details? Prices, that kind of thing?"

"Not over the phone. If you're interested, the next stage is for you to come in and have a chat. We can go over the details with you then."

"That sounds great. When can I do that? I'm very keen to get started."

"You're in luck. We've had a last-minute cancellation for six pm today. Could you make it then?"

"Sure. No problem."

I gave her my 'made-up' pixie details, and she gave me directions to their office.

***

Before I embarked on my pixie adventure, I had an appointment to keep with Jordan Rice's estranged wife, Sandra. When I'd contacted her, she'd been less than enthusiastic about speaking to me, but in the end, I'd managed to guilt-trip her into sparing me a few minutes for the sake of Amy Rice.

Sandra Rice still lived in the family home; a modest semi-detached house on the outskirts of Washbridge. I parked on the road outside her house. The blue Fiat on the driveway was a few years old, and in need of some bodywork. She must have been keeping a lookout for me because she answered the door before I had time to knock.

"Jill Gooder?"

"Err—I—err—yeah, that's me."

I know what you're thinking: Jill can't even remember her own name now, poor girl. In fact, I was a little taken aback because as soon as I saw Sandra Rice, I realised that I'd seen her before—her and her car. She was the woman who had been captured on the restaurant's CCTV. The woman who had arrived a few minutes before Gordon Rice, and then left just before he did.

"Are you okay?" she asked.

"Sorry, yes. I just had a funny turn. It must be low blood sugar."

"Go through to the lounge. I'll make us both a cup of tea."

There were photographs of Sandra and Jordan on the sideboard.

"Are you sure you wouldn't like a biscuit?" She offered the biscuit tin again. "What about your low blood sugar?"

"It's okay. I'm fine now, thanks." I had absolutely no desire to eat her *contaminated* biscuits: Ginger nuts and chocolate digestives in the same tin? What was she thinking?

"I'm sorry if I came over as reluctant to help. Amy is a lovely person; I can't imagine what she's been going through."

"That's okay. I just want to ask you a few questions about your husband."

"Sure."

"Do you mind telling me why the two of you have separated?"

"Jordan's gambling is out of control. I've lost track of the number of times that he's promised to stop, but he can't. He spent all of our savings and more. I couldn't take it any longer, so I told him he had to move out."

"Is that the only reason?"

"Yes."

"Are you sure about that?"

"What are you getting at?"

"I know that you met up with Gordon Rice on the day that Douglas died."

"That's nonsense."

"It was captured on the restaurant's CCTV."

"Oh no." She lowered her head.

"How long have you been seeing one another?"

"For about three months."

"Did Jordan find out? Is that why he moved out?"

"No, he doesn't know anything about it. And, he must never find out."

"What would he do if he did?"

"Jordan has a temper."

"Has he ever been violent towards you?"

"No, but he's come close to it a few times."

"Was Gordon with you all the time you were at the restaurant?"

"Yes, of course. Why?"

"Are you sure about that? He didn't nip out—just for a few minutes?"

"No. We were together all the time."

Sandra Rice was still shaken when I left her. She was no doubt worried that her husband might find out about her affair with his twin brother. The question was, had she lied about Gordon? Had he been with her all the time they were at the restaurant, or was she covering for him?

**

It had been over an hour, and Maddy was still working on me. Shrinking to 'pixie' size had been easy enough, but that was only the start. Maddy had got me to try on several of her outfits before finally deciding on the green dress. And then there was the hair and makeup.

She took a few steps back to admire her handiwork.

"You'll do," she pronounced with less enthusiasm than I'd hoped for.

"Will they believe I'm a pixie?"

"Yeah." She nodded. "I think so."

She wasn't exactly filling me with confidence.

"It'll have to do. If I don't go now, I'll be late for the appointment."

"Good luck, Jill."

I had a feeling I was going to need it.

The address I'd been given was a small office in the commercial sector of Pixie Central. The door had nothing on it other than a number, and there was no sign outside to indicate who or what was inside. I was getting increasingly bad vibes about this.

I tried the door, but it was locked, so I knocked. The sound of footsteps confirmed there was someone in there. Moments later, the door was unlocked, and a pixie, dressed in a smart pinstripe suit appeared.

"Yes?"

"Flo Feathers." It was the name that Maddy and Lionel had come up with for me. They'd insisted that 'Jill' wasn't sufficiently pixie-like.

He glanced up and down the corridor, presumably to check I hadn't been followed. "Come in."

The only furniture in the tiny office was a desk and two chairs.

"I'm Frankie Forest. Please take a seat."

"Thank you." Inwardly, I gave a sigh of relief. I appeared to have passed the 'pixie' test.

"What made you decide to contact us, Ms Feathers?"

"I've always been fascinated by humans, and the human world. It is my greatest desire to go there—to live there. That's why I joined the Human World Society."

"You're somewhat older than the other students I've seen from the college."

Cheek! "I'm a mature student."

"I see."

"How much do you know about our organisation?"

"Only what people at the society have told me. I believe you can make it possible for pixies to live in the human world?"

"That's correct, but I should warn you that it doesn't come cheap. The fee is one thousand pixie dollars."

"That's fine." I had no idea what the exchange rate between human money and pixie currency would be, but I could worry about that later.

He spent the next thirty minutes quizzing me about my background and my reasons for wanting to live in the human world. Fortunately, I'd spent some time with Maddy and Lionel practising my responses to all the questions I was likely to face.

"Okay, Ms Feathers. I'm very pleased to confirm that I am able to offer you a place on the Human Experience."

"Really? That's fantastic!"

"You'll need to report back here tomorrow at two pm. And bring the cash with you."

"Tomorrow?"

"Is that too early for you?"

"No, tomorrow is fine. Do I need to bring anything else?"

"No." He stood up. "Just one final thing. You mustn't tell anyone what you are doing, or where you are going. Not even friends or family. Is that clear?"

"Crystal. I'll see you tomorrow."

Chapter 23

I'd changed back into my own clothes, reverted to human size, and magicked myself back to Washbridge. At least the Robbie Riddle case was looking a little more promising now. That was more than I could say for the other two cases I was working on. Had Gordon Rice killed his older brother? The CCTV coverage of him entering the factory was pretty damning, and yet Sandra Rice still insisted that he'd never left the restaurant. His apparent lie about the phone call he'd received from Douglas was also working against him.

As for the other missing person case, I had so far drawn a blank. When I'd first discovered that Brendan Bowlings was having an affair with his secretary, I'd thought I was onto something, but having spoken to Sarah Weller, I was convinced she was as much in the dark about what had happened to Brendan as everyone else. The only other lead I had on that case was from the fisherman who had said he'd seen Bowlings that day. According to Tommy Brakes, Brendan had said he was going to try to get to his old fishing spot—inside the fenced off area. It was time to get out my wellingtons, and take a closer look at the fence around the anonymous factory at Wash Point.

I planned to start where the fence cut across the river, and work my way all around the perimeter. Brendan had told Tommy Brakes he knew of a way to get through the fence, so maybe there was a gap somewhere.

After thirty minutes, I hadn't found any gaps or holes in the fence, but I had found a section that looked to have been recently repaired. Could Bowlings have got through the fence there? It was possible, but that didn't explain what had happened to him. I needed to get inside to take a look around.

While I was still considering which spell to use, I took out my phone to check the time. It was switched off. I'd forgotten to switch it back on when I'd left BeHuman. As soon as it powered up, it began to beep. I had twelve missed calls: Nine from a number I didn't recognise, and three from Kathy. What was going on?

"Kathy? You've been trying to get hold of me?"

"Jill. Thank goodness. Is Jack okay?"

"Jack? Yeah, I think so. Why?"

"Haven't you seen the news? There's been some kind of shooting incident at a jewellery shop in West Chipping. It said that there had been at least one fatality. It's probably nothing to worry about, but I thought I should—"

I ended the call, and immediately rang the other number that had been trying to get hold of me. It was West Chipping police station, but I didn't get a human being—I was in a queue. My hands were shaking, but I managed to end the call, and bring up the local news on my news app. The headline was stark: 'Shootout at Jewellers. At least one dead—several injured'.

I quickly skimmed the article. Police had been called to a robbery gone wrong at a jeweller in West Chipping. Shots had been fired. Three people, including at least one police officer, had been taken to West Chipping Hospital. There was thought to be at least one fatality.

It would take me at least thirty minutes to drive there, and I wasn't even sure I'd be able to manage it because my hands were shaking. I would have to magic myself over there.

***

Please let him be okay. Please.

I rushed to the reception desk. "Where are the people who were brought in after the shooting?"

"No one is allowed to go through—"

I didn't have time to waste, arguing. Fortunately, I spotted a familiar figure. Dougal Andrews, a reporter at The Bugle, was remonstrating with a police officer in the corridor to my right. Andrews was trying to get past, but the officer wasn't having any of it. I slipped into the loo, cast the 'invisible' spell, and then hurried towards the corridor. Dougal was still arguing as I made my way past him and the police officer.

"Jack?" I'd reversed the 'invisible' spell, and was checking each of the curtained cubicles.

"You can't come in here." A nurse blocked my way.

The man on the bed was surrounded by medical staff. The doctor was working frantically to save him. I managed to get a look at his face. It wasn't Jack.

The next cubicle was empty.

"Jack?"

The third cubicle contained a similar scene to the first. Doctors and nurses were working on another man. I tried to get a look at his face, but this time my view was blocked.

"Jill?" A hand touched my shoulder.

I spun around to find Jack standing behind me.

"What are you doing here? How did you get in?"

I threw my arms around his neck, and broke down in tears.

"Let's get out of their way." He led me back along the corridor, past Dougal Andrews who was still arguing with the police officer, and out of the building.

"I thought you were dead," I blubbered. "Why didn't you call to tell me you were okay?" I thumped his arm.

"Sorry, I should have, but I was too busy worrying about Craig."

"Who's Craig?"

"My partner. He took a bullet, but they said he's going to be okay."

"The news report said there had been a fatality?"

"That was the perp. He turned the gun on himself."

"Are you sure you're okay?"

"I'm positive. What about you. Are you alright to drive?"

"I didn't drive here. I — err — Kathy gave me a lift. Yeah, I'll be fine. You get back to Craig."

After Jack had gone back inside, I found a quiet corner, and broke down in tears again. I cried for what felt like forever.

My phone rang. It was Kathy.

"He's okay," I managed. "He wasn't injured."

"Thank goodness. What about you?"

"I'm okay. Now."

***

Jack and I had only been together for a relatively short time, but I now couldn't imagine my life without him. For a while there, I'd been terrified that I might have lost him. I was always quick to ridicule Jack for worrying about me, but I'd just been given a taste of how it felt. And I didn't like it.

It was still early, but the last hour had left me physically and mentally drained, so I decided to call it a day. I magicked myself back to the car, and then drove to Smallwash.

There was a car parked on the driveway next door. A couple, probably in their early thirties, were just emerging from the front door. I wasn't really in the mood for small talk, but the woman spotted me, and waved.

"Hi!" she called, and they both made their way over.

"Hello there." I somehow managed a smile. "Checking the place out?"

"Yeah. It's ideal. We saw it a few days ago, but by the time we called the agent, it had already been let. Then yesterday, I got a phone call to say the tenant had changed his mind after being here only a few days."

"That's right."

"Sorry, we should have introduced ourselves. I'm Clare, and this is Tony."

"Jill Gooder. I live here with Jack."

"Is there anything we should know about the house, Jill?" Tony said. "We're a little concerned that the previous tenant quit so quickly."

"No. There's nothing to worry about. It was a student who moved in — I think he decided that he'd prefer to live closer to the college. That's all."

"That's great." Clare looked delighted. "We do love the house. I guess we'll soon be neighbours, then."

Tony and Clare certainly looked normal enough. They were definitely a much better proposition than Worm, and his all-night parties.

"Are you okay, Jill?" My mother's ghost was waiting for me inside the door.

"Mum! You scared me to death."

"Sorry, but I heard about the shooting incident, and wanted to make sure you were okay."

"I'm fine." I lied. I still felt pretty shaken.

"Is Jack okay?"

"Yeah. He wasn't injured—thank goodness."

"I wish you two didn't have such dangerous jobs."

"You don't have to worry about us, Mum. Especially not me. I have magic to fall back on."

"Magic doesn't make you invincible or immortal."

"I know, but like I said, I'm okay." I could see my mother was upset, so I had to get her off the subject. "I've been trying to travel to Ghost Town."

"That's not possible, is it?"

"I didn't think so, but there's a rumour that Magna Mondale may have done it. I gave it a try the other day with Mad, but it didn't really work."

"What happened?"

"Mad called my name from GT, and I tried to cast a spell that would get me to her."

"I wouldn't even know how to begin to do that. Your magic certainly has come a long way in a short time. How did it go?"

"Not particularly well. I seemed to get stuck in some kind of void. I'm probably just wasting my time."

"What about if I was to call you from GT?"

"How do you mean?"

"We're family. We share the same blood. Maybe, if I called your name, you'd be able to get over to me."

"I'm not sure if that's a good idea."

"What do you have to lose?"

"I guess we could give it a try."

"Okay. I'll go back there now, and then I'll call your name."

I wasn't very optimistic, but I cast the spell and waited. Moments later, I sensed my mother calling to me. I focussed as hard as I could on her voice.

The sensation was beyond weird; I felt as though I'd been caught up in a tornado—everything seemed to be spinning.

And then I landed with a bump.

"Jill? You did it!"

"Mum?" I appeared to be standing in a kitchen.

"Well done, Jill! That was incredible!"

"Whose house is this?"

"It's mine. Whose do you think it is?"

"And you?" I stared at her. "You look different. You look—"

"Alive?"

"Yeah. I suppose so."

"I only look like a ghost when I make an appearance in the human world. Here in GT, I look—err—normal, I guess."

As I walked over to the window, I still felt a little unsteady on my feet. "It looks just like the human world."

"What were you expecting?"

It was a good question. "I don't know. Something more—err—ghostly."

"How do you feel?"

"Okay, I think. Can I go outside?"

"I don't see why not." She led the way to the front door.

I couldn't get over how normal everything looked. The row of houses opposite wouldn't have looked out of place in Washbridge. "That must be Dad's house."

"See what I mean about the colour? It lowers the whole

tone of the neighbourhood. Do you want to go over and say hello?"

"Not just now. Getting here took its toll, and I'm not sure how easy it's going to be to get back."

"Okay, but now you know you can do it, you have no excuse for not visiting regularly."

"I will. I promise."

We made our way back inside, and I set out trying to get back to the human world. My first two attempts failed miserably, but on the third try, I landed with a bump back in the hallway of my house.

I'd just about composed myself when Jack walked through the door.

"How is Craig?" I said.

"He's fine. Just a flesh wound. They're keeping him in overnight for observation, but he should be home tomorrow."

"That's good news." I gave him a kiss. "Now, you and I are going to bed."

Chapter 24

Jack feigned shock when he walked into the kitchen, the next morning. I'd been slaving away for thirty minutes, making a full English breakfast for both of us, and although I say it myself, it looked and smelled pretty darn good.

"Are you feeling okay, Jill?"

"Just don't get used to it."

"I'll have to get shot at more often if this is what I get."

"Don't you dare. My heart can't stand another shock like yesterday."

"This doesn't look bad at all." He smirked. "Considering you made it."

"Cheek. I expect you to eat all of that. By the way, I saw our new neighbours yesterday."

"Already? That was quick."

"They seem pretty normal. I don't think we'll have any all-night parties with those two."

"Oh, I just remembered." He stood up, and began to walk towards the door.

"You haven't finished your breakfast."

"I'll only be a minute." I heard him go outside, and then open and close the car boot. "Look what I've got." He opened the small white box.

"A gold condiment set? Nice."

"Do you like them?"

"They're shaped like parrots."

"I know. Great, aren't they?"

"Gold parrots?"

"You don't like them, do you?"

"They're—err—great. I'm sure your parents will love them." Always assuming they have no taste whatsoever.

Mrs V was manning the office by herself.

"Jill. Did you give any more thought to the 'G' situation?"

"Sorry, Mrs V, I've been really busy. When is she coming over?"

"Later today. I don't know what I'm going to do if she says she wants to move in."

"Don't panic just yet. I still might be able to sort something out."

"I'd be eternally grateful, if you could, Jill."

The good news was that all the small origami models had been removed from my office. The bad news was that they had been replaced with a number of giant ones: three swans, a rose and something that looked like a snail.

"There's hardly room to swing a cat in here, Winky."

"Just as well."

"Where did you get the giant sheets of paper from?"

"Origami Paper Supplies."

"I hope you didn't pay for it with any of my cards."

"Fret thee not. I used some of the money I've made on gym membership subscriptions."

"Just don't make any more, or my clients won't be able to get through the door."

"Clients?" He laughed. "Good one."

Twenty minutes later, Mad called into the office.

"What's with the paper swans and flowers?" She weaved her way around them, to my desk.

"The cat has taken up origami."

Mad knew me well enough by now not to be surprised by that revelation.

"I have good news," she said. "I've tracked down the items that were stolen from the colonel."

"That's great."

"What do you want me to do with them? Shall I bring them here, so you can return them to him?"

"Actually, I have something to tell you first."

"Oh?"

"I managed to transport myself to GT, yesterday."

"How did you manage that?"

"I used the same spell as I did with you, but this time my mother called my name. Somehow, that seemed to do the trick."

"Wow! That's great!"

"I was surprised by just how normal GT is. Even my mother looked normal."

"I had the same reaction the first time I went over there."

"I need to keep doing it. Hopefully, with practice, it'll get easier like it did with magicking myself to Candlefield. The first few times I did that, I thought it was going to kill me. Nowadays, I don't give it a second thought."

"Why don't you give it a go now? If it works, we can pay a visit to the thief together."

"Haven't you done that already?"

"No. I was waiting to see what you wanted to do."

"Okay. You go first, and I'll try to follow."

This time, it was so much easier.

"That's brilliant!" Mad said. "This is going to be great."

"Shall we go and get the colonel's property back?"

"First, why don't I introduce you to my contact at the police station?"

"Isn't that Aubrey?"

"No. He's in overall control. I'm talking about Constance Bowler. She's the detective I liaise with most of the time."

"Is that a good idea? I don't have a very good track record with the police. Maxine Jewell isn't my biggest fan, and Leo Riley—well, the least said about him, the better."

"Connie is different. The two of you will get on like a house on fire."

Mad led the way to the police station. I was fascinated by GT. It could have been any town in the human world, but I was still finding it hard to come to terms with the idea that all of its residents were ghosts.

We only had to wait a matter of minutes at reception before we were joined by a woman who looked to be about forty years of age. Although, to be truthful, I wasn't sure how meaningful age was when it came to ghosts.

"Hi. I'm Connie Bowler."

"Jill Gooder."

"Sorry if I'm staring. I can't quite get my head around the idea that you're actually here in GT."

"That makes two of us."

We went through to Connie's office where tea and biscuits were served. The tea tasted just the same as it did in the human world, but I was disappointed to see that there were no custard creams on offer.

"This could be really big," Connie said. "There's been a lot of inter-world crime between the human world and GT. Until now, it's been difficult to stamp out, but if you're willing to work with us, I'm sure we could make an impact."

"If I can help, I'll be delighted to, but I have to be honest. I'm not used to getting such co-operation from the police. I'm persona non grata with your counterparts in both the human and sup worlds."

"That definitely isn't the case here. I hope that we'll be able to help one another."

"Funny you should say that," Mad chimed in, and then brought Connie up to speed with the theft of the colonel's property.

"Glad to help," Connie said. "This can be our first case working together."

Less than fifteen minutes later, we were in what was no doubt the less salubrious part of GT city centre. The block of flats was run down, and smelly.

"Ready?" Connie said, in a whisper.

Both Mad and I gave her the thumbs up.

For a petite woman, Connie packed a punch. Or in this case a kick. The door yielded to the second blow.

Inside, a scruffy-looking man with bad teeth and very little hair, seemed shocked at our sudden appearance.

"Hello, Viggo," Connie said.

"There was no need to break down my door, Mrs Bowler."

"I know you, Viggo. If I'd knocked, you'd have done a runner out the back door."

"No, I wouldn't. I'm always pleased to see you, Mrs Bowler. Who are your—?" He stopped mid-sentence when his gaze landed on me. "She's not a ghost. Not a para neither."

"This is Jill Gooder." Connie made the introductions.

"She's a witch."

"That ain't possible."

"Apparently, it is." Mad walked towards him. "She's come to collect some items which you stole from a friend of hers."

"I don't know what you're talking about. I ain't stolen anything."

"You won't mind if we take a look around then, will you?" Connie didn't wait for a reply.

Half an hour later, we had recovered all the items on the colonel's list, and Connie had taken Viggo in, to face charges.

"Thanks for this, Mad," I said.

"My pleasure. This new ability of yours is going to make such a difference."

"I hope so. I'll return these to their rightful owner, but before I go, do you mind if I ask you another favour?"

"Why not? It's not like I don't owe you."

"My PA has a problem."

"Which PA? You have so many."

"Touché! It's Mrs V. Her sister is talking about moving up here; she wants to live with Mrs V."

"I take it Mrs V isn't very enthusiastic?"

"No, and I don't blame her. Her sister, Mrs G, is a nightmare."

"Mrs V and Mrs G? Really?"

I nodded. "Mrs G is always putting Mrs V down. She's a nasty piece of work."

"How can I help?"

"I need you to give her the same kind of performance as you gave my noisy neighbour."

"Is that all? No problem. I know a few ghosts who get a

great kick out of scaring humans. Let me have all the details, and I'll get onto it."

***

The colonel was delighted to get his property back, but I was forced to decline his and Priscilla's offer to join them for dinner. I needed to get to Maddy's house, so she could give me the 'pixie' makeover again, ahead of my 'Human Experience'.

I was a few minutes late getting to the rendezvous point; Frankie Forest was tapping his watch when I arrived.

"You're late."

"Only a couple of minutes, sorry."

"Do you have the cash?"

I handed over the pixie dollars that Rhoda Riddle had given me.

After counting it, he ushered me onto the minibus which was human size, but which had six small seats fitted into the back. I joined the other three pixies — all males — who were already inside. Frankie Forest obviously wasn't travelling with us. He had a few words with the driver, a wizard, and then waved us on our way.

"Hi, I'm Neil." The pixie seated next to me introduced himself.

"Flo Feathers. Do you know how all this works?"

"No idea. It's all very hush-hush. Are you nervous?"

"A little."

The seats were too low to see out of the windows on the side of the bus, but I was able to see out of the window in the rear door. After a few miles, it became apparent that we were en route to Washbridge. I suppose I should have expected that. The Human Experience was bound to take place in the human world. But where?

We came to a halt, and I could hear the driver pressing keys on a number pad. Moments later, he drove through a set of metal gates, and into the grounds of a small factory. Even before he allowed us to get out of the vehicle, I realised where we were. It was the anonymous factory at Wash Point.

We were led inside by a wizard, wearing a white coat. He took us to a room, which had been fitted out with pixie-sized desks and chairs. When we were all seated, another wizard appeared through a door to our right.

"Welcome to the Human Experience. You are here because you want the opportunity to live in the human world — something which is normally impossible to do as a pixie." He gestured to someone at the back of the room, who turned off the lights. "This brief video will show you the process. Before you view it, I should emphasise that it is totally painless, and entirely safe." With that, he started the video which displayed on a large screen at the front of the room.

"Any questions?" he asked, once the presentation had finished, and the lights were back on.

"Are you sure it's safe?" Neil asked.

"Absolutely. We've been doing this procedure now for some time without any issues. Any more questions?"

"When does it happen?" I asked.

"Tomorrow morning at nine am, so I suggest you all retire to your rooms where you'll find a meal waiting for you. There's a TV and DVDs for your entertainment. Please make sure you get a good night's sleep. You must not, under any circumstances, leave the accommodation area until you are collected in the morning."

From there we were taken to our accommodation which comprised individual, self-contained rooms not unlike those found in budget motels.

What I had seen on the video had horrified me. BeHuman had developed a means of changing a pixie into human form. The process was part magic, part chemical engineering. At least now I knew why they had positioned the factory to include the river in its grounds. The transformation process took place inside metal pods which became extremely hot. The river water was diverted into the factory where it was used to cool the pods during the two-hour long process. Taking that much water from the mains would have been very expensive. This way they were able to cool the pods without incurring additional costs, and the water wasn't polluted in any way. The video had shown a pixie climb into one of the pods, and then climb out, two hours later, as a human. Impressive? Certainly. Scary? You better believe it.

What about Robbie Riddle? Where was he? And where were the other two missing pixies? According to the video, pixies who transformed into human form would still be able to return to Candlefield because, although they may appear to be human, they were still essentially sups. If that was the case, why hadn't Robbie returned to Candlefield? He must have known his family and friends would be worried about him. Had something gone wrong? Was there something we weren't being told?

It was time to find out.

Chapter 25

First, I reversed the 'shrink' spell to bring myself back to human size. Next, I cast the 'invisible' spell to enable me to explore the building without being observed. I made my way to the laboratory where the transformation process would take place. It was an elaborate set-up with four metal pods suspended from the ceiling. Below each of the pods were metal channels through which water flowed. I knew, from having viewed the video, that the pods were lowered, the pixies climbed into them, and then the pods were submerged in the water. When the process was complete, the pods were raised out of the water, and the pixies were taken out of them—now in their human-like bodies. During the induction video and talk, they had gone to great lengths to make it clear that the pixies would be sups inside a human 'shell'. They would not actually be humans.

From the laboratory, I made my way along several corridors, and checked inside a number of offices, but didn't see or hear anything of particular interest until I heard a voice.

"Let me out! I won't say anything, I promise. Please, let me out!"

I followed the sound until I came to a door with a small window; inside was a wizard, with long unkempt hair.

When I reversed the 'invisible' spell, he jumped back in shock.

"Who are you?" He was visibly shaken.

"Never mind that. Why have you been locked in there?"

"Because I threatened to blow the lid on this bogus operation."

"What do you mean? Blow the lid, how?"

"Who are you?"

"I'm the person who will get you out of there, if you tell me everything you know."

"How do I know I can trust you?"

"You don't, but what other options do you have?"

He hesitated. "Okay. The transformation process works fine most of the time, but in a small number of cases, there's a delayed side-effect."

"What kind of side-effect?"

"The pixies seem okay when they leave here, but there have been reports of at least three of them falling into a coma."

"That's some side-effect." I remembered the article I'd read about a number of unknown coma patients in Washbridge Hospital.

"I tried to persuade them to call a halt to operations until we'd found out why it was happening. When they refused, I said I was going to the Candlefield press. That's when they locked me in here. Now, can you get me out?"

"Stand back. I'm going to use the 'power' spell."

"That won't work. I've already tried that. You have to find the key."

"Stand away from the door."

He looked doubtful, but did as I said.

The door proved to be no match for me once I'd cast the spell.

"How did you do that?" He looked stunned.

"There isn't time to get into that now. What's your name?"

"Max Blackstone."

"Do you think you can find your way out of the factory without anyone seeing you, Max?"

"Sure. I know my way around here like the back of my hand."

"Good. Get going then."

"What about you?"

"I still have work to do here."

He started down the corridor, but then stopped. "They're holding a human prisoner."

"Who?"

"I don't know. Someone they found in the grounds, I think. "

"Where is he?"

"I'm not sure, but I've heard him calling out, so he can't be far away."

"Okay. Get going!"

I checked every other door along the corridor. At the fifth one, I found what I was looking for. A human was sitting on the floor of the room.

I knocked on the glass. As soon as he saw me, he hurried over to the window.

"Get me out of here!"

"Who are you?"

"My name is Brendan Bowlings. I'm being held captive. Can you get me out?"

"Yes, but you'll need to stand back from the door."

Once he was clear, I forced it open.

"How did you manage that?"

"There's no time to explain. Take my hand."

He looked puzzled, but did as I asked. I magicked both of us to a stretch of the river upstream from the factory. Before he could ask any awkward questions, I cast the 'forget' spell, and made my escape while he was still dazed. He'd remember his captivity, but the spell should ensure he had no memory of me or how he got away. I was pretty sure he would already be on his way to contact the police, so I had to act fast.

I made a call.

"Daze? I need your help, and I need it now."

"What's wrong?"

I gave her a quick rundown on what I'd discovered, and she promised to be with me within fifteen minutes. At my request, she was going to bring plenty of backup.

While I waited for Daze to arrive, I played back the two cases in my mind. Brendan Bowlings must have found a way to get inside the fence, and had been captured and held prisoner ever since. What they eventually planned to do with him was anyone's guess.

There was little doubt that Robbie Riddle had undergone the transformation to human form. What was less clear was what had become of him since then. He was obviously close to his family and friends, so why hadn't he been back to Candlefield to visit them? Was he afraid they would be too shocked by his appearance, or had he been one of the pixies who had suffered side-effects? My instincts told me it was probably the latter.

"Okay. What's the plan?" Daze was ready for the fray.

"The human who was being held prisoner in there is probably on his way to the police, so they could be here at any moment. If you and your guys can get everyone inside the factory back to Candlefield before the police get here, that would be great. The three pixies inside the accommodation area are innocent. Everyone else will need to face justice for what they've done. Oh, but if you come across a wizard named Max Blackstone, you should go easy on him. He did work here, but he tried to put a stop to the operation when he realised that things were going wrong. He was being held captive too. I let him out earlier, so he may already have made it back to Candlefield."

"Okay, will do. What are you going to do?"

"I need to find those three coma victims. One of them could be the pixie I've been trying to locate. I'm not exactly sure what I'm going to do when I find them, though."

"If the process is at least partially magic, it's quite possible the wizards on the medical staff at Candlefield Hospital will be able to treat them. If you can magic the coma victims back there, I'll warn the hospital staff that you're coming."

"That sounds like a plan."

***

Before I entered Washbridge Hospital, I had a couple of dry runs at magicking myself back and forth between there and Candlefield Hospital. I wanted to be sure that I was able to land in the area that had been set aside for our arrival, where several mattresses had been laid out on the floor, to provide a soft landing for the incoming patients.

All three coma victims were in the high-dependency unit. There were several members of staff around, but no one was actually beside the beds. By making myself invisible, I was able to get to each bed in turn, to confirm that despite appearances, they were all sups.

I was going to attempt something I'd never done before: to magic someone who was unconscious back to Candlefield with me. I took hold of the hand of the first man, and cast the spell. Moments later, we touched down safely on the mattresses. While the medical staff took the first patient away on a trolley, I repeated the process for the other two. Phew! Success! And not a moment too soon because a nurse was headed towards the beds — she was in for something of a shock.

The fate of the three pixies was now in the hands of the wizard doctors in Candlefield Hospital.

**

I had an appointment with Mr Twoday at the offices of Day, Day, Day, Day & Week, solicitors.

"You have Magna Mondale's book, I see," he said. His forehead was just as shiny as on our previous meeting.

"I do." I placed it on his desk.

"Would you mind if I take a look?"

"Help yourself."

He examined the book for a few minutes, pronounced himself satisfied that it was the genuine article, and then handed it back to me. "I won't be a minute." He left the office for a short while, and then returned carrying a small book. "This is Imelda Barrowtop's journal. I'll need you to sign for it if you wouldn't mind?"

The journal was roughly A5 in size. Once I was back outside, I couldn't resist taking a quick look at it. The contents of the first page read:

Magna has asked me to keep this journal, and to record everything which happens to her. Although I readily agreed, I did ask her why she didn't record it in a diary of her own. She told me that she feared that if something was to befall her, the diary might be taken or destroyed. No one would suspect that I might be keeping a journal on her behalf. She plans to contact me on a regular basis, and to bring me up to date on events, so that I may record them. The journal is to be passed on to whoever presents him or herself to me, bearing Magna's book, which she has today sealed in a room in the basement under her house. I asked who that person might be, but she insists she does not know. In the event of my death, I have left instructions in my Will relating to this journal.

There were literally hundreds and hundreds of pages of entries, and I could see from only a cursory glance that they did not cover every single day. In some cases, there were periods of days or even weeks between entries. I read the first few pages, but there was nothing of any particular significance. In fact, much of it was mundane: Magna went to the market place, Magna took tapestry classes, that kind of thing.

It was going to take a long time to read it all, and right then, I had other more pressing matters to attend to.

***

Mrs V was busy winding a ball of wool when I got back to the office.

"Any messages?"

"Nothing for you, but I've had some good news." She beamed. "You know I asked you if you'd try to think of a way to stop G moving in with me?"

"Yes?"

"Well, you don't need to bother. She's packed up her stuff and gone home. And what's more, she says she's never going to spend another day in my house."

"That is good news. What made her change her mind?"

"You'll never believe it. That crazy sister of mine insists that she saw ghosts in my house. I think I'd know if I had ghosts. She'd probably been at the sherry. Anyway, I don't care. It means that I don't have to worry about that now."

"That's great news, Mrs V. I'm very pleased for you."

Well done, Mad.

Chapter 26

A man couldn't be in two places at once. And yet, Gordon Rice had been captured on CCTV going into his factory at the same time as he was supposedly in a restaurant with Sandra Rice. It was always possible that Sandra had lied, but my gut told me that wasn't the case.

I brought up the short clip of CCTV, from the petrol station, that I'd saved to my phone. After playing it back and forth several times, I was just about to give up on it when I spotted something. As the man came into view and walked over to the front door of the industrial unit, he did so with a slight limp. It was nothing too pronounced, and could easily have gone unnoticed—I'd already missed it several times. But it was definitely there. To the best of my knowledge, Gordon Rice did not have a limp, but Jordan, his twin brother, did.

Eureka!

If my hunch was right, Gordon Rice had not been in two places at the same time. When his brother was murdered, Gordon had been in the restaurant with Sandra. Jordan Rice was the one who had gone to the cold storage unit, and was most likely the murderer.

But how to prove it?

I drove straight over to the unit, but parked a couple of streets away. From there I made my way on foot. The door wasn't locked, so I quietly let myself in. So far, so good, but where was Jordan?

A banging noise led me to him. He was working in the room which contained the large freezer in which Douglas Rice had met his untimely end. This was the ideal place to put my plan into action.

"Doug!" Jordan screamed. "It can't be you."

He'd just seen what looked to him like his dead brother. I'd had to rely on the photograph of Douglas Rice when casting the 'doppelganger' spell, but judging by Jordan's reaction, it had worked okay.

"Surprised to see me, Jordan?"

"Leave me alone!" He began to back away.

"I can't do that. You killed me, so I intend to haunt you for the rest of your life."

"It's just my imagination playing tricks on me. You're not real."

I reached out, and touched his arm. He flinched and moved away.

"Does that feel real to you, Jordan?"

"Leave me alone!"

"Why did you do it?"

"To get back at Gordon. He stole the only thing that ever mattered to me."

"Sandra? You had lost her long before she and Gordon got together. Your gambling drove her away."

"We could have got back together. We could still have made it work. Until Gordon made a move on her."

"If it was Gordon you wanted to hurt, why kill me?"

"If I'd killed Gordon, they would have known I'd done it. No one would have believed you'd murdered him; you're too nice. I had no choice. I knew they'd have no trouble believing that Gordon had murdered you."

"You killed me because I was too nice?" I shook my head in disbelief.

"I'm sorry."

"Don't give me that. You planned all of this. You wore

the black T-shirt and jeans so they'd think you were Gordon, and you followed Sandra to the restaurant. You knew about the CCTV, so you parked out of sight, didn't you?"

"Shut up! Leave me alone! I didn't know what I was doing. My head was messed up."

"It wasn't messed up when you bought a burner phone, called Gordon, and pretended to be me, was it?"

"I've said I'm sorry. Won't you just leave me alone?"

"Were you planning to sell the business, with both of us out of the way? To fund more of your reckless gambling?"

"No! Leave me alone!" He rushed past me and out of the building.

Jordan Rice probably thought he could escape the ghost of his dead brother if he managed to get away from the scene of the murder.

But he was wrong.

I magicked myself over to his bedsit, to ensure that I got there before he did. I made myself invisible, waited for him to arrive, and then sneaked in after him. He headed straight for the kitchen, where he grabbed a half-full bottle of whisky. He didn't bother with a glass; he just downed a long drink straight from the bottle. When he turned around, he came face-to-face once again with what he assumed was his brother's ghost.

"No!" the glass dropped from his hand, and smashed on the floor. "Leave me alone!"

"I did warn you. I'll be with you all the time from now on."

"Please, no! I'm sorry. I'll do anything."

"Anything?"

"Yes. Please just go away!"

"Give me your phone."

He handed it to me, and I made a call.

"Detective Riley, please. Tell him it's about the freezer death case. Someone wants to confess to the murder." While I was waiting to be connected, I turned to Jordan. "If you confess to murdering me, then you won't see me ever again."

"You promise?"

"Cross my heart."

"Riley speaking. What's this all about?"

I handed the phone to Jordan, who couldn't wait to make a confession.

***

The next day, Jack was behaving like a cat on hot bricks.

"I wish you'd settle down." I took a sip of orange juice. "Your pacing up and down is doing my head in."

"I'm nervous about today."

"Why are you nervous? I should be the one who's nervous—meeting your parents for the first time."

"I just want our families to get on well together."

"They will. Kathy and Peter can get along with anyone. Aunt Lucy is a love. And the twins might be a bit giddy, but they won't cause any problems. Just thank your lucky stars that Grandma isn't coming. That would have been a different kettle of fish altogether."

"I still don't understand why she couldn't make it."

"I told you. She's going to a conference. She couldn't get out of it."

He began to pace up and down again; it was starting to

make me dizzy.

"Why don't you read your paper?" He'd been out at the crack of dawn to buy a loaf of bread and a newspaper.

"I've already read it from cover to cover. I'm so pleased I got transferred out of Washbridge. There's some weird stuff happening here."

"Such as?" I grabbed The Bugle. The main headline read: *'Coma victims disappear'*.

I skimmed through the article.

"That is weird," I said.

"No kidding. It was strange enough that no one knew who they were, but for them to just disappear into thin air? That's mega weird. And then there's the guy who was held captive in that factory at Wash Point."

The second headline in The Bugle was: *'Missing man claims he was abducted'*.

"According to this article, the man didn't know why he was being held, or even who was holding him," I said.

"We may never know. By the time the Washbridge police got down there, the place was deserted. Everyone had scarpered."

"Any idea what was going on inside the factory?"

"No one seems to know."

The minibus was coming to pick us up just after midday. Aunt Lucy and the twins were the first to arrive. After everyone had said their 'hellos', and I'd made us all a drink, Aunt Lucy pulled me to one side.

"Rhoda Riddle called me this morning. Robbie is awake and sitting up in bed."

"That's great. Is he still human-shaped?"

"No. They managed to reverse that pretty quickly,

apparently. Rhoda asked me to thank you."

"I'm just glad Robbie is okay. Did she say whether he'd told her anything about what happened to him?"

"Just that he didn't want anything to do with the human world ever again."

I laughed. "Probably just as well."

"The police have arrested the pixie behind it — someone called Frankie Forest."

"Good. I hope they throw the book at him."

"They've also arrested Barnaby Bandtime from the Human World Society. Apparently, he was getting a kickback for every student he sent to BeHuman."

"That explains why he was so hostile when I went to see him."

Kathy and Peter arrived a few minutes later.

"I'm really looking forward to today," Kathy followed me into the kitchen.

"I'm not. What if his parents don't like me?"

"He'll just have to dump you." She laughed. "Of course they'll like you."

"How's Peter?"

"He's really pleased with life. Have you heard about that factory at Wash Point?"

"I saw it in The Bugle."

"Pete reckons they'll close it down, so he might get his favourite stretch of river back."

Just then, my phone rang. "Sorry, Kathy. I need to take this." I went out into the back garden.

"Jill? It's Amy Rice."

"Hi, Amy."

"Have you heard about Jordan?"

"Yeah. I saw it in The Bugle."

"I can't believe it. From what the police have told me, Jordan wanted to get back at Gordon for having an affair with Sandra. Why did he have to kill Doug? It doesn't make any sense. I hope they lock him up and throw away the key."

"Have you heard what's happened to Gordon?"

"They've released him. He's going to come over here later this week, so we can discuss what to do with the business. Anyway, I just wanted to let you know, and to ask you to bill me for the time you've spent on this."

"Thanks for calling. I'll get my invoice out to you."

***

While we were waiting for the minibus to arrive, everyone was chatting—everyone except me. I'd sneaked upstairs to have another quick look through the journal. Most of it was still fairly routine stuff. I was beginning to wonder why Magna had bothered to ask Imelda to keep it, but then I stumbled across this entry:

Magna says she saw him again. The man with the red hair and beard. She thinks he's following her.

My blood ran cold as I recalled the man who had followed me. The man with the red hair and beard who I'd found dead in a cupboard close to my office. The man called Damon.

"Jill!" Jack called from downstairs. "The minibus is here."

"You lot go ahead. I'll be down in a minute."

I desperately wanted to read more of the journal, but it

would have to wait. I hurried downstairs and out to the bus. Everyone was already on board. The driver, a young woman, greeted me when I boarded.

"Hi, I'm Dee Ryver."

"Hi. I'm Jill. Sorry to keep you waiting." I took the seat next to Jack.

We'd only travelled a few hundred metres when the bus came to a halt.

"Is everything okay, Dee?"

"There's an old woman, flagging us down."

Oh no!

"Shall I let her on?"

"Yes, you'd better," Aunt Lucy shouted before I had a chance to yell, 'drive on!'

"Grandma?" I said. "I didn't think you were coming."

"I wasn't going to, but then I got to thinking. What kind of party would it be if I wasn't there?"

Oh bum!

ALSO BY ADELE ABBOTT

The Witch P.I. Mysteries:

Witch Is How... (Books #25 to #36)
Witch is How Things Had Changed
Witch is How Poison Tasted Good
Witch is How The Mirror Lied
Witch is How The Tables Turned
Witch is How The Drought Ended
Witch is How The Dice Fell
Witch is How The Biscuits Disappeared
Witch is How Dreams Became Reality
Witch is How Bells Were Saved
Witch is How To Fool Cats
Witch is How To Lose Big
Witch is How Life Changed Forever

The Susan Hall Mysteries:
Whoops! Our New Flatmate Is A Human.
Whoops! All The Money Went Missing.

AUTHOR'S WEB SITE
http:www.AdeleAbbott.com

FACEBOOK
http://www.facebook.com/AdeleAbbottAuthor

MAILING LIST
(new release notifications only)
http:/AdeleAbbott.com/adele/new-releases/

Printed in Great Britain
by Amazon